DASTAAN

-E-

ISHQ

A Love Saga

AARHAAN S. BHATTI

DASTAAN -E- ISHQ

Dastaan -e- Ishq

DASTAAN -E- ISHQ

Dastaan -e- Ishq

By: Aarhaan S. Bhatti

This is a work of fiction. Names, characters, businesses, places, events, and incidents are either the product of the author's imagination or used in a fictitious manner. Any resemblance to actual persons, living or dead, or events is purely coincidental.

Cover design by Aarhaan S. Bhatti

Imaging By Dall-E

Edited By Aarhaan S. Bhatti

Printed in USA

ISBN: 9798312002553

DASTAAN -E- ISHQ

DISCLAIMER

Dastaan -E- Ishq A Love Saga is a work of fiction. All characters, events, and locations in this book are products of the author's imagination and are used fictitiously. Any resemblance to actual persons, living or dead, or to real situations or agencies is purely coincidental.

The author prohibits the replication, reproduction, or utilization of any material, including but not limited to plots, characters, or situations, by any media, television or film agencies, or organization without written consent.

The story is a condensed narrative that portrays a situation through a series of emotional experiences. The events are purely fictional. Characters' interpersonal situations do not reflect real life, living, or deceased individuals. Situations related to the story are purely fictional and are not intended to represent or harm any personal morals, culture values, or religious sentiment.

The opinions expressed in the novel belong to the characters and should not be confused with those of the author. The names, characteristics, and places depicted in this story, including the titular 'Dastaan -E- Ishq,' are entirely the author's creation and are not intended to represent specific individuals, public offices, events, situations, or locales, whether historical or contemporary.

This book is a work of fiction and should be regarded as such. Any perceived similarities to real-life circumstances or entities are unintended and incidental. The author does not represent or is represented by any company, corporation, or brand mentioned herein.

DASTAAN -E- ISHQ

DEDICATION

For those who dared to dream, to feel, and to love!

To my family and friends who inspire me every day to be a better version of myself.

DASTAAN -E- ISHQ

Table of Content

DASTAAN -E- ISHQ

ACKNOWLEDGMENTS

I extend my deepest appreciation to all those in my life; providing wisdom, feedback, and support were invaluable throughout this creative journey. Your insights and encouragement fueled my determination to see this project through.

A special thanks to the dedicated professionals—editors, designers, and all those behind the scenes—whose expertise and dedication to transform this manuscript into a polished work.

Lastly, to the readers, your passion for storytelling and curiosity makes every word worthwhile. Thank you for joining me on this adventure; sharing these stories with you is an honor. May this book bring you joy, transport you to distant realms, and kindle the fires of your imagination.

DASTAAN -E- ISHQ

ACT ONE

In the heart of Lahore, nestled within a quaint town, Kasim Ali Chaudhry lived a life that, on the surface, seemed perfect. Born into the esteemed Chaudhry family, led by his influential father, Rehan Chaudhry—a distinguished lawyer—Kasim was raised to embody grace and charm. Yet, beneath this carefully curated façade lay an insecure soul, burdened by concealed dreams and an innate fear of the world and its expectations.

When Kasim looked in the mirror, he didn't see what others

saw—a young man with striking features. Instead, he perceived a distorted image shaped by his insecurities. His struggle with weight was more than just physical; it was a psychological battle that dictated his self-worth. He didn't see anything special about himself. His inner voice projected, calling him mediocre. Despite his kindness, humor, and warmth, he was his own harshest critic, unable to appreciate his strengths. Behind the mask of joviality, he carried a reservoir of unspoken dreams stifled by the shadows of self-doubt.

Although he harbored aspirations, Kasim hesitated to acknowledge his own potential. The weight of self-doubt kept him from embracing his dreams fully, holding him back from the life he yearned for. As a devoted son, he prioritized his father's wishes above his happiness, an act of filial obedience that inadvertently became a barrier to his personal fulfillment.

Each morning, as dawn bathed the city in golden light, Kasim began his day with a quiet ritual centered around his childhood companion and neighbor, Ruhaniya Khan— though she preferred to be called *Ruhi*. She lived life on her own terms, made her own rules, and was often ruled by her fiery temper. Her heart, carefully hidden from the world, seemed visible only to Kasim.

Beneath the sharp edges of her personality, he knew she cared deeply for the people she loved. Her fearless passion for life brought unexpected color to Kasim's otherwise dull, routine existence.

And so, each morning, as he stood by his window, toothbrush in hand, his eyes instinctively searched for her. The balcony door opened, and there she was—emerging into the morning light as the golden rays of the sun kissed her fair complexion.

Ruhi, being a young attractive woman in her mid-twenties, possessed an effortless grace. Her long, flowing black hair cascaded over her back as she dried it with a towel on her balcony.

Her doe eyes sparkled with mischief as they locked onto Kasim's across the space that separated them. His heart skipped a beat. Their connection was silent yet undeniable.

With a knowing smile, Ruhi picked up her dry-erase board and scrawled a message. "What's the plan?" She held it up for him to see.

Kasim, still brushing his teeth, hesitated before shrugging. "Not sure," he gestured.

Ruhi, undeterred, scribbled back. "Let's go see a movie."

Enchanted by her spontaneity, Kasim quickly nodded and wrote a simple "Okay."

But just as their moment unfolded, the tranquility shattered. The doors of their respective houses swung open, and their fathers stormed out, voices rising in fury.

"I will not spare him today!" Omar Khan, Ruhi's father, bellowed.

"Today is the day I put him in his place!" Rehan Chaudhry, Kasim's father, roared.

Once inseparable childhood best friends, Rehan and Omar had become bitter enemies over the years, their bond severed by an old, unspoken tragedy. Their daily clashes had become routine, fueled by petty grievances—chief among them, the positioning of their cars in front of their homes.

Omar Khan, a well-respected physician in Lahore, lived a simple life with his wife and daughter. Despite his prominence, he had always valued humility over wealth. Rehan, burdened by his family's legacy, wore his pride like armor—often clashing with Omar's grounded, no-nonsense attitude.

As their heated argument spilled into the street, their wives—long accustomed to these dramatic encounters—tried, in vain, to intervene. Eventually, exasperated, they withdrew, leaving their husbands to their endless bickering.

But Kasim and Ruhi, despite the public animosity between their families, knew better. While the world believed them to be distant, they remained best friends, navigating the turmoil of their fathers' feud secretly.

Together, they stepped forward, using their well-practiced diplomacy to calm the situation. After much persuasion, they managed to pull their fathers back inside, restoring the usual uneasy truce.

As the morning chaos settled, Kasim returned to his routine, standing before his mirror, rehearsing words he had long yearned to say. Today, he told himself, will be the day I finally tell Ruhi the truth.

He had loved her for as long as he could remember. Yet, every time he resolved to confess, doubts crept in like shadows, whispering reasons to hold back.

Ruhi was different. She was fearless, full of life, and driven by dreams that reached far beyond the confines of their neighborhood. She was meant for greater things, and that both awed and intimidated him. He thought.

Will she ever look at me the way I looked at her?

Or I'm destined to remain just the guy next door—the childhood friend who loved her from a distance, too afraid to take the leap?

Kasim was drawn to Ruhi's ambitious spirit and unwavering confidence, yet the deeper layers of her character truly captivated him. He admired her profound understanding and her kindness to those around her. Even though the world sometimes misinterprets her outgoing nature as superficial, Ruhi possesses a heart of gold. Her love for her family—and for his—remained unshaken despite the long-standing feud between their fathers.

Ruhi remained a beacon of warmth and love in the intricate tapestry of their intertwined lives. While their fathers' grievances sought to drive a wedge between their families, she refused to let history dictate her relationships. Her connection with Kasim's family endured, unbothered by the bitterness between the elders.

As Kasim contemplated confessing his feelings, he grappled with his own fears and the reality that Ruhi, though living in her vibrant, ambitious world, deeply valued the bonds of family and friendship. He stood at the edge of vulnerability today, ready to step into the unknown and redefine their relationship.

The rhythm of his morning continued as he descended the stairs for breakfast, only to be met with his father's ever-critical gaze. Rehan Chaudhry was a man of habit and discipline, and he wasted no time directing his disapproving remarks toward Kasim—his weight, academic performance, and perceived shortcomings. Each word settled heavily on Kasim's shoulders, tainting the start of his day.

Kasim's older brother, Daniyal, was the peacemaker. Aware of Kasim's emotional struggles, he bore their father's criticism out of respect. His love for Kasim ran deep, and he often wished his brother would stand up for himself. Daniyal recognized Kasim's potential and respected his desire to forge his path.

Daniyal always offered a voice of reason. Stepping in, he urged Kasim to focus on his aspirations rather than their father's harsh judgments. His support, a rare respite amid the criticism, injected a fleeting moment of encouragement.

Yet, the household remained tense as father and son clashed in a silent battle of expectations and defiance. Seizing an opportunity, Kasim quickly left the house, escaping the weight of the conversation that had already drained him.

Stepping into his car, he drove a few houses down—where Ruhi awaited. Their morning carpooling ritual was an unspoken pact, a shared secret. Shielded from their families' watchful eyes, the drive to university was a sanctuary, a brief escape from the expectations that bound them.

As they drove, Ruhi immediately sensed the sadness in Kasim's eyes. She knew his father must have said something hurtful again. Kasim was a man of few words, quiet and enigmatic to most—but not to her. She understood him

8

without needing an explanation. Without hesitation, Ruhi squeezed his hand, offering him a smile.

Kasim knew what she meant. *It'll be fine.*

He returned the smile, grateful for her silent reassurance, and quickly changed the subject. He asked about her preparations for the upcoming university talent show, where she was organizing a fashion show.

Excitement lit up Ruhi's face as she shared her grand plans. But Kasim's heart sank when she casually mentioned that Imran would be her showstopper.

Imran—the college heartthrob, the notorious Casanova.

As Kasim watched Imran interact from a distance, he couldn't help but see through the persona Imran had crafted to impress others—a façade layered with manipulation and narcissism. He wondered why Ruhi couldn't see past the mask. Still, Kasim found quiet solace in knowing he was nothing like him. He was aware of his flaws—he wasn't particularly good-looking, overweight, and only an average student—but Kasim knew one thing for certain: he was kind and genuinely cared for others.

Kasim was genuinely happy for Ruhi's success, but an unsettling discomfort gnawed at him. He concealed his unease with a faint smile, unwilling to voice the emotions brewing beneath the surface.

As they arrived on campus, Kasim cautiously broached the topic, expressing his doubts about Imran's trustworthiness. But Ruhi brushed off his concerns with a confident smile, chalking it up to his usual protectiveness.

"He's a nice guy, Kasim," she reassured him. "You should give him a chance."

Their disagreement remained unspoken, lingering between them. But as Kasim parked the car, the tension escalated. Imran stood nearby, waiting for Ruhi, his presence thickening the air. Kasim watched as Ruhi's demeanor shifted—her attention fully diverted toward Imran, leaving Kasim feeling like an outsider.

Imran barely acknowledged Kasim's existence, offering nothing more than a cold shoulder before leading Ruhi away. Kasim stood there for a moment, invisible in their wake. Without a word, he turned and walked away, the sting of the moment settling in his chest.

His father's expectations, Ruhi's shifting priorities, and the uncertainty of his future weighed on him as he made his way to class.

Then, a teacher's voice interrupted his thoughts.

"Dean Iqbal wants to see you."

Kasim's steps faltered.

Inside the office, reality struck harder than he had anticipated. His grades in pre-law and political science were dangerously low. The principal's message was clear: unless he improved immediately, he risked being dismissed from the university.

But there was an alternative.

Recognizing Kasim's strength in sciences—biology, and chemistry—the principal suggested a shift in focus. The choice was his: either struggle to keep up with a field he didn't love or pursue what truly came naturally to him.

For the first time in a long while, Kasim felt clarity. He agreed to enroll in additional biology courses, a step toward a different path—one he had always been drawn to.

Yet, he chose to keep this decision a secret.

Telling his father that he was struggling in college was not an option. Their family legacy of lawyers was on the line. So, he carried the burden alone, determined to navigate this path without disrupting his family's fragile expectations.

That evening, Ruhi approached him with a request—she needed his help with the fashion show. Kasim, eager to spend time with her, readily agreed. He imagined an evening where it would be just the two of them, a moment of ease amidst the chaos of his life. They quickly departed for the movies, but his hopes were dashed when Ruhi invited the rest of her friends—including Imran.

Kasim swallowed his disappointment, masking it behind a neutral expression. As they settled into their seats at the movie theater, laughter filled the air—Ruhi's laughter, directed at something Imran had said. Kasim sat silently, smiling faintly, concealing the hurt that simmered beneath the surface.

As Kasim and Ruhi return home, their hopes for a lighthearted evening are quickly shattered. The tumultuous sight of their fathers engaged in yet another heated argument greets them on the street, their angry voices echoing through the neighborhood.

Yells and accusations fill the air, casting a shadow over the night. Alarmed, Kasim and Ruhi rush forward, attempting to intervene and understand the cause of the latest confrontation.

Rehan Chaudhry, his anger barely contained, accuses Omar Khan of slashing his car tires. He insists the tire was perfectly fine that morning, fueling his suspicion that Omar is to blame.

The altercation quickly spirals beyond a mere flat tire, unearthing years of unresolved grievances. Old wounds resurface, turning the mundane incident into another battleground for their families' bitter history.

As the argument escalates, Rehan's fury erupts. His voice shakes with emotion as he hurls accusations at Omar and his family, calling them liars—and murderers. The weight of his words hangs thick in the night air before he storms inside, leaving behind a stunned silence.

Kasim and Ruhi, caught in the crossfire of their fathers' relentless feud, are left grappling with the echoes of a past that refuses to let go.

Inside, Kasim follows his father and, with quiet determination, pleads with him to let go of the past. But Rehan, his eyes dark with rage and grief, refuses. Kasim and Daniyal's pleas are unheard by their father. His wife, shattered by the events of the day, cries as she states that it's a misunderstanding and that her sister-in-law would hurt herself because of Omar's brother.

Kasim pleads again, "Abba, you have to let this go."

Rehan ignores him as Daniyal steps forward. "Abba, we don't know what happened to her. It could've been an accident."

"It was no accident. I was a lawyer even before you were born. I'll never forgive them for what they did."

His voice cracks as he bellows, "The day my dead sister comes back to life is the day I'll let go of the past!"

The pain in his words is unmistakable. He turns to Kasim with a bitterness that has hardened over two decades.

"Her death is Omar's fault. His family's fault." And with that, he walks away, leaving Kasim in the silence of an unresolved tragedy.

The following days bring an uneasy calm to the household. They returned to their normal lives, but the event left all of them with open wounds. Omar found comfort in his wife's company, thinking about the past.

"I think we should go there and clear this misunderstanding," Kiran said calmly.

Omar smirked. "He's not going to listen."

"But we have to try," Kiran said with tears in her eyes.

"Why Kiran? It's been twenty years." Omar said, his frustration evident in his hurt. "If he cared enough, he would've given me a chance to explain myself. I'm not going to beg him."

"What we're going to do, let this keep going on?" Kiran's voice was laced with emotional turmoil.

"Yes. And I suggest you tell Ruhi to stay out of this." Omar said as he left abruptly.

While at Rehan's residence, emotions are running high. Rehan sits in the family room in the evening, deep in discussion over a court case with Daniyal when Kasim enters. Immediately, Rehan's attention shifts, his gaze sharp with disapproval.

"Have you thought about your career yet?

Are you going to do something with your life…. I want you to finish college this year and enroll in law school as soon as you can.

I *don't* know what you're doing—" Rehan prods.

Kasim remains silent.

"I can't keep telling you…"

Rehan's frustration against Kasim rapidly grew with each passing day. Daniyal calms his father down by placing his hand on his knee.

Displeased, Rehan pivots to another familiar source of

criticism—Kasim's weight.

"Have you seen yourself in the mirror? You're moping around all day.

Only god knows what you're doing in college.

Do you think anyone will want to marry you when men your age are fit and successful?"

A heavy silence blankets the room. Kasim leaves, heading upstairs.

Daniyal intervenes, "Abba. How many times have I told you to please let him be?"

"I'm his father. I'm worried about him?" Rehan responds with irritation.

"*Abba,* you have every right to worry, but constantly body shaming him or becoming aggressive is only going to push him away further," Daniyal said calmly.

Rehan said as Reshma entered, "I didn't have any problems with you."

"Abba, we're different people. You don't need to compare both of us."

"Because your Abba just needs a reason to fight with someone these days. If he's not laying into Kasim, he's fighting with Omar across the street." Said Reshma.

"Come in; please go ahead and advocate for your son." Said Rehan sarcastically.

"Yeah, why wouldn't I? He's doing everything he can. Has he ever given you any reason to be disappointed in him?" asked Reshma.

"He hasn't yet. But he will if he continues this path." Said Rehan.

"What path is that exactly?" Said Reshma.

"A path of destruction. He's attending college, but I'm noticing he's not focused.

When Daniyal was his age, he already started law school." Rehan said angrily.

"Daniyal finished his college two years early. So, what if it's taking him a little longer." Said Reshma.

"Of course, you're going to side with your son. I have to show my face in society and answer questions when my peers ask me about him." Said Rehan.

"No one is telling you to answer. Tell people he's studying." Said Reshma.

Daniyal grew tired of this conversation.

"*Ma*, please, let's not escalate this conversation further."

"You tell your mother it took years for you to make your life. People see determination in a man to assess suitability for proposals.

Have you seen your son?

He walks around looking like a homeless person. No direction in life.

No career.

No passion for *anything*.

He's overweight. And he *doesn't* care for his health.

You think anyone would give us their daughter for him…

Have you ever said to him *this is the time to take care of yourself, Kasim.*" Said Rehan.

"You just need a reason to put him down." Said Reshma.

Daniyal, sensing the growing tension, interjects.

"Let him find his own path, Abba.

He's an adult. He doesn't have to be who *you* want him to be."

Rehan, unmoved, shakes his head. His expectations remain unwavering.

Just as the conversation nears its boiling point, Reshma, their mother, shifts the focus to another pressing issue—the inability of Mahirah, Daniyal's wife, to conceive.

"What about you, Daniyal?"

"What about me?" Daniyal interjected.

"If people are asking your father about Kasim. People are asking me about you and your wife." Reshma said, her tone fueled with anger.

"*Ma,* it's really *not* about me or Mahirah," Daniyal said as he tried to defuse the situation.

"Your father should know how I feel when people question me about you, too, and why your wife hasn't conceived." She said, releasing her anger.

"Ma, *please,*" Daniyal said, hoping his mother would let go of this as Mahirah entered.

"Ma—" said Mahirah.

"Oh, I'm glad you're here. You should listen to what everyone is saying." Reshma's sharp tongue cuts through Mahirah's heart as she stands there quietly.

"Every time I go out to any event, everyone asks me.

Daniyal and Mahirah have been married for two years, and they haven't conceived yet.

Is there something wrong with Mahirah?

Have you gotten her checked?

Oh, here is my OBYN's number; she's great…

Do you know how I feel, Rehan?" said Reshma with tears in her eyes.

"Both of these situations are different, Reshma." Said Rehan as he noticed his daughter-in-law's silent tears.

Reshma's coldness toward Mahirah deepens, pushing her to retreat upstairs in tears, with Daniyal following in support.

"No, I'm just trying to explain to you.

If you have expectations from your sons, then I can also have expectations from my daughter-in-law." Reshma said angrily.

"Do you hear yourself?

I want my son to advance in his life.

His career.

Daniyal *will* become a father one day, but you have no right to humiliate Mahirah like that, especially in front of her husband and father-in-law…

You know well as I that it's *not* her fault—" Said Rehan as Kasim entered.

The revelation lingers in the air, laden with unspoken disappointment.

Kasim stepped forward, defending his brother and sister-in-law.

"Ammi, let it go. Some things are not in our hands."

Reshma, though hesitant, nods as she absorbs his words. The weight of societal expectations—constant whispers about the absence of grandchildren—has consumed her. But now, she sees the truth in her son's plea.

Determined to make amends, she heads upstairs, where Mahirah finally confides in Daniyal about her fear of being a disappointment.

"Why don't you divorce me?" said Mahirah, crying.

"Why would I do that?" Said Daniyal.

"So, you can give your mother the happiness I can't," said Mahirah.

Reshma listened in silence as she made her way upstairs to their room. Her shame quickly gave way to grief, the weight of her own words crashing down on her with the full force of their cruelty.

"What's wrong with you, Mahirah?

Every day, you say the same thing. Aren't you happy with me?" Daniyal asks with sincerity.

"I've never been so happy in my life. Who wouldn't want a husband like you?

Who takes care of my every need.

Who listens to me?

Ask me about my opinion. I'm lucky to have you, but….

But I *can't* ignore how your heart breaks when I tell you I had *another* negative pregnancy test.

My heart breaks when I see you smile and say, 'It'll have next time.'

I watch you at the stores…looking at newborn clothes and

shoes. You'll pick it up and leave it, which really shatters me from the inside.

I know how much you want this, and believe me, I want this for you more than I want this for myself." Mahirah said, bursting into tears.

Reshma's heart breaks listening to the conversation as shame and remorse set in.

"I hate it when women come up to you and ask you about why you're not pregnant yet.

How they look at you…judging you.

I hate it when they put their hands on your stomach and say, 'Oh no, don't worry about it. It'll happen one day inshallah'.

You're right. I do want this, but—" Daniyal said, comforting her.

Mahirah pleads with Daniyal.

"Then divorce me and marry another so your parents can get the happiness they deserve."

"I'll *never* do that. I married you; you're my first love and last.

You'll be my first wife and my only wife.

You're enough for me.

You hear me.

If god doesn't bless us with a child, we'll be enough for each other."

"But—"

Daniyal, unwavering in his love, takes her hands. "You will always be the mother of my children, whether they exist or not.

I didn't marry you to leave you in our hard times.

The day you said yes to me; you made me complete. Besides, a child is just a bonus…

And don't worry about Ma; she loves you a lot."

"I know she loves me a lot and didn't mean it. She's—"

Unbeknownst to them, Reshma watches from the doorway. Overcome with emotion, she steps in, placing a hand on Mahirah's shoulder.

"I raised a good son," she says softly. "And I was wrong to make you feel anything less than family."

Mahirah hugged her instantly. "No, Ma."

"I'm so sorry; I don't know what got over me. I should've understood you're in pain, too." Reshma said as her voice broke a little.

"No, Ma, it's   " Mahirah said, holding her tears back.

"What I said was not okay.

But you have to know this, I will never let my son leave you so he can have a child with another woman.

And if he does, he's *dead* to me.

You can't break a home to make another with someone else.

How can you be happy if you do that?" Reshma said wiping Mahirah's tears.

"You must promise me you'll never tell him to leave you. I brought you home to make our family complete.

And you're a perfect daughter.

God didn't bless me with a daughter because he was supposed to send you into our lives.

I'll pray for you to become a mother as long as it takes. I'm done worrying about others or what they'll say. We'll wait for this miracle to arrive as long as it takes." Reshma continued as she kissed Mahirah's forehead, and Daniyal hugged her.

***

Ruhi was exhausted by the constant tension between the two households. Her first instinct was to escape, to distance herself from the daily conflicts that had become an unavoidable part of her life. She longed for the days when both families lived in harmony and when they could visit each other's homes without fear of consequences.

But deep down, she knew things would never return to how they once were—unless someone took a stand. It was time to speak to her father, to urge him to let go of his vendetta before it consumed them all.

As Ruhi confronts her father, tension crackles in the air at Khan's household. Her voice is firm yet pleading.

"You and Rehan Uncle were best friends once," she reminds him. "Isn't that worth something?"

Omar scoffs, unmoved.

"Let it go, Ruhi!"

"Abu. Every day, there's something new. The whole neighborhood is getting tired of this."

"Stop caring about others. These people need some sort of

entertainment…I suggest you let go of this and focus on your studies. This is your last year."

Ruhi ignores him.

"The death of Rehan's sister wasn't anyone's fault, Abu. It's been twenty years. When will you let it go?"

But Omar's eyes darken. "Never," he says, his voice low. "Even when the truth comes out, you'll understand why."

Ruhi watches him, stunned by the weight of his words. Whatever secrets lie buried between their families, her father has no intention of letting go.

As night falls, Ruhi and Kasim retreat to their balconies, their private sanctuary. Beneath the starlit sky, she gazes upward, lost in thought. Kasim, however, only watches her. His heart flutters with joy as he secretly glances at her, with her eyes on the night sky.

He picks up his dry-erase board and writes, "Situation diffused."

Ruhi smirks before responding by writing on her dry-erase board, "For now."

They both know their parents' war is far from over.

Ruhi then shifts the conversation, scribbling on her board. "You have to help me with the show."

Kasim hesitates. He can't tell her about his extra classes, about the pressure mounting on him. So instead, he simply writes, "Okay."

The burden of time weighs on him, but as Ruhi waves goodnight and disappears inside, he buries his worries behind a smile.

Kasim's life turns into a relentless cycle of sleepless nights—balancing premed studies while helping Ruhi with the talent show. But he never complained. He pulls all-nighters, determined to fulfill both his academic and personal commitments. Then, an unexpected arrival shakes things up.

Ruhi's cousin, Saira, visits Khans as her parents are out of the country. Saira's arrival was unexpected but hopeful, as Kasim had another friend to talk to openly. Saira's fond of Kasim and his family, as she's known them for years.

When the two neighbors were friends twenty years ago, Rehan helped Omar arrange Saira's parents' wedding. When Saira visits the Chaudhry house, Rehan surprises everyone by greeting her warmly and placing a blessing hand on her head.

Despite Omar's watchful gaze, Rehan silently withdraws inside. Saira meets the rest of Rehan's family and quickly returns to her uncle's house. Rehan heads upstairs; he remembers how Reshma and his departed sister Asma cared for all these kids. Saira, being the youngest, got all the attention. His memories of the screaming, happy children filled his heart with joy.

Behind closed curtains, he watches Saira with a bittersweet smile as sorrow in his heart latched onto him. For a split moment, he wished things were as they once were, their family's best of friends.

But it was a dream that'll never come true.

"It still can happen," Reshma said as Rehan secretly watched Saira and Ruhi on the lawn from his window.

Rehan's remorse takes charge of his emotions.

"It's too late, Reshma."

"It's never too late." Reshma pleads yet again.

Rehan breaks down. "I can't get her out of my head. Her lifeless body in my arm."

"It's not their fault," Reshma interjects.

"But it *is*. She took her own life. Because Omar's brother left her for someone else at the last minute.

How can I forget that?

Tell me, was twenty years enough for you to forget her."

Reshma wipes her husband's tears. "I remember her every day. But I *can't* accept she took her own life. Asma wasn't a coward."

"Omar's brother's betrayal turned her into one. I'll never forgive him.

I never thought my best friend, who was like my brother, would betray me like that.

I thought my bond with him was deeper than blood. In the

end, he sided with his brother and let my blood spill in the process."

Reshma, however, challenges his narrative.

"You and Omar pushed them into that marriage without asking her.

She agreed to the wedding for you.

Even after Noman called off the engagement, she *was* happy for him.

Your sister was trying to move on. She had accepted it her fate."

Rehan remains firm. "Nothing can change the past. *Asma wasn't happy.*

I used to hear her cry upstairs, hiding from all of us. Since she was a kid, she held her pain inside with a smile on her face.

Reshma, my sister was heartbroken, and that's why she took her life *because of them.*

I'll NEVER forgive Omar for his part in this." Said Rehan, exiting.

His voice echoed in Reshma's ears as she watched Ruhi and Saira laugh together; something flickers in her eyes—a quiet longing for what was lost.

Maybe one day… things will be as they were years ago.

The day turned into evening, and with his extra classes and talent show preparation, Kasim hardly got time to run errands. Kasim quickly realized his exams were near, and he hadn't even gotten his books. His swiftly wipes his sweat off his head as his heart races thinking about his exam's outcome. His hope for a better future seemed distant.

Kasim quickly headed out to buy books from a local bookstore. However, his eyes catch the attention of a premed course book he picks up to view as he unexpectedly runs into Omar.

Seeing the books, Omar embraces him warmly, pride evident in his voice. Kasim's phone rings, displaying his father's call, which he swiftly declines.

"I'm glad to see you here…Ah, premed. This is a very good book. The author is one of my old colleagues." Omar said, analyzing the book.

"It's nothing. I'm taking some science course, so I was just looking for a quick review." Kasim said, leaving the book on the shelf.

"Look, Kasim, you're a smart kid. You should explore your options. There is a world outside of law and political science."

"You know Abba—"

"Your Abba once wanted to become an actor but quickly realized it wasn't for him."

"He wanted to be an actor?"

"It was a phase, not a passion. Whatever you do, make sure you're passionate about it."

Silence roamed the store as Omar remembered his good times with Rehan.

"Kasim, life is too short to live up to someone else's

expectation. I know you love your father. But be true to yourself, too.

Whatever path you choose, make sure it's your own," Omar tells him.

Kasim only nods. He doesn't reveal his struggles, but Omar offers silent understanding.

"Regardless of me not being on a good term with your father, I do care about you and your brother very much. If you need anything from me, all you have to do is just ask.

I know you'll find your way. I believe in you." Omar as he left the store.

The encouragement he received from Omar felt great, as he never received this encouragement from his father.

The following day, when he arrives at the university, Ruhi questions him about why he didn't pick them up earlier in the morning, to which Kasim explains that he had some errands to run. She quickly switches her focus to pressing matters.

She greets him with a task list for the fashion show. He

secretly hopes—just for a moment—that she will ask him to participate. But instead, she informs him that the ramp lineup is final, with Imran as the showstopper.

Kasim swallows his disappointment and smiles. He had hoped she would at least ask him to be in the show, if not the showstopper. Saira notices his inner sorrow but remains quiet.

Kasim quietly continues helping Ruhi, hoping she'll notice his hard work in making the set. However, she chose to spend her time working on the project, training Imran for the show.

That night, Ruhi taps on his window with pebbles, asking if he got the fabric designs. He confirms, hoping to spend time with her; he asks her if she wants to get some ice cream. She ignores his plea and coldly responds that she has plans with Imran.

Overwhelmed by jealousy, Kasim walks away without a word. Ruhi watches him go, puzzled by his reaction—unaware of the storm brewing within him.

In the days that followed, Kasim deliberately distanced

himself from Ruhi. His avoidance was intentional, a silent protest against the growing presence of Imran in her life. Confused by his sudden coldness, Ruhi struggled to understand what had gone wrong. The once effortless connection between them had now turned into a strained silence.

Sensing the shift, Saira took it upon herself to guide Kasim through the final preparations for the fashion show. But even as she did, she couldn't ignore the underlying tension between Kasim and Ruhi. Their absence from each other's lives created a noticeable void that did not go unnoticed by those around them.

Imran, ever opportunistic, seized the moment. With Kasim withdrawing, he stepped in effortlessly, showering Ruhi with attention and filling the space Kasim had left behind. Their growing proximity was like fuel to a fire, stoking Kasim's anger further. Unable to stomach their closeness, he made a resolute decision—he would stop talking to Ruhi altogether.

The silent rift cast shadows over the final days leading up to the fashion show. What was once an unbreakable friendship now felt fragile, burdened by unspoken emotions and jealousy. Neither confronted the issue, allowing misunderstandings to take root and fester. The question lingered—could their bond survive the weight of everything left unsaid?

The night of the fashion show arrived, dazzling with energy and excitement. The event was a resounding success, marking a milestone achievement for Ruhi. Her talent and hard work paid off when she was offered an internship with a renowned fashion designer in Karachi—a dream opportunity. Simultaneously, Imran secured a modeling contract in the same city, setting the stage for a new chapter in their lives.

Instead of immediately sharing the news, Ruhi decided to keep it a secret. She wanted to surprise everyone with the announcement, choosing to celebrate the victory with those closest to her. That night, she arranged a dinner to reveal her big plans, inviting friends and family to share her joy.

But Kasim was absent.

His empty seat at the table gnawed at Ruhi, fueling the frustration building within her for weeks. She tolerated his indifference, avoidance, and unexplained distance—but tonight, it felt like too much. His absence on such an important night felt like a betrayal.

Disheartened and angry, she returned home, her emotions bubbling dangerously close to the surface. Unable to contain her frustration any longer, she stormed onto her balcony. Her eyes locked onto Kasim's window, her patience unraveling completely. Without thinking, she picked up a small rock and hurled it at the glass. The sharp sound of shattering glass pierced the quiet night.

Startled by the sudden crash, Kasim rushed outside, his heart pounding. He looks through his window, shattered glass everywhere. He glances at Ruhi, who points him to come downstairs. As he stepped onto the street, he found Ruhi standing there, her arms crossed, her eyes burning with frustration.

"What the hell, Ruhi?!" he snapped. "You just broke my window! Are you mad?"

Ruhi barely flinched. "I was *this close* to throwing a brick," she shot back, her voice dripping with exasperation.

Kasim rubbed his temples, trying to keep his cool. "You realize you could have just *called* me instead of waking up the entire neighborhood?"

Ruhi glared at him. "Oh, now you care about *talking*. Now you suddenly have something to say?"

Kasim let out a sigh, knowing exactly where this was going.

Ruhi stepped closer, her frustration giving way to something more vulnerable. "I'm tired of this, Kasim. You've been ignoring me, avoiding me, acting like I don't exist. And for what? What did I do?"

Kasim hesitated, torn between anger and the truth that had been clawing at his heart for weeks.

Ruhi took a deep breath, her voice quieter now. "I needed you tonight. And you didn't show up."

Her words struck him harder than he expected.

For a moment, neither of them spoke. The night air was thick with everything they had left unspoken.

Kasim clenched his jaw. "Maybe you don't need me as much

as you think you do…. And you should've called instead of making a scene."

Ruhi's eyes flickered with hurt, but she masked it quickly.

"I should've called you," Ruhi muttered, breaking the silence first.

"Yeah, you could've," Kasim replied coolly.

"Really?" she scoffed, her frustration bubbling over.

"What's your problem, Ruhi?" Kasim asked, exasperated.

"You know very well! Stop playing games," she snapped.

"What *is* your issue?" Kasim asked, his patience thinning.

"I don't understand why my best friend wouldn't support me on the biggest night of my life!" Ruhi exclaimed.

Kasim furrowed his brows. "What are you talking about?"

"My fashion show, Kasim!"

He let out a dry laugh. "You making no sense. The show went great.

What's the problem now?"

"You've been distant for weeks! You didn't even come to dinner tonight. It was *important*," Ruhi said, her voice softer but filled with hurt.

"That's what this is about?" Kasim asked, shaking his head.

"I can't believe this," Ruhi said, anger flaring again. "You're doing this because of your jealousy."

Kasim scoffed, looking away. "Go upstairs, Ruhi. And go to sleep; clearly, you're tired."

"I'm seeing through you; you're jealous."

"And you're delusional."

"No, I'm not. I see things more clearly than ever." She took a step closer. "You're *jealous of my success.*"

Kasim's jaw tightened. "You *really* think that?" His voice was low, dangerous.

"Yeah, I *truly* believe it… Just because *you* can't amount to anything, you're taking it out on me," Ruhi said coldly.

"Whatever, Ruhi," Kasim turned to walk away, but her next words stopped him.

"Go ahead, walk away—just like you always do. Just like you're walking away from *everything* in your life!"

Something inside him snapped. He turned back, rage flickering in his eyes.

"Is that what *you* really think of me?"

Ruhi held his gaze, her arms crossed, unwilling to back down.

"If you *truly* believe that," he continued, his voice trembling with restrained emotion, "then you're a bigger fool than I thought.

You've changed!"

Ruhi unfolds her arms as she points to herself.

"I changed?

Me?"

"Yeah," Kasim said, stepping closer.

"How?" Ruhi asked, her voice sharp as ever.

"Now that Imran's your whole world, no one else exists."

Ruhi groaned. "I *don't* understand your rivalry with him!

Why are you so insecure?

Is it because he's better-looking than you?

Or.

Because he's popular and you're not?"

A humorless chuckle escaped Kasim's lips. He clapped slowly, his eyes shimmering with unshed tears.

"I expected that from *everyone*—but not from *you*."

Ruhi sighed. "It's *true.*"

Kasim shook his head in disbelief. "So that's how you see *me*," he whispered. *"Like I'm nothing."*

She didn't answer.

"You're a fool, Ruhi," Kasim said softly, a sorrowful smile

on his lips. *"You can't even see what's right in front of you."*

Ruhi furrowed her brows. "And what exactly am I not seeing?"

Kasim's heart pounded. His fingers curled into fists at his sides. His breath hitched.

"That I'm in love with you!"

Silence.

For a split second, Ruhi looked shocked. Then, to his horror, she *smiled* in disbelief.

Kasim felt his heart crack.

"You *think* you're in love with me," she said gently, shaking her head.

His stomach twisted. "What?"

"You *think* you're in love with me, but you're *not*," she repeated.

Kasim stared at her, every fiber of his being breaking apart. "I've been in love with you since we were kids," he whispered.

Ruhi sighed, her expression soft but firm.

"*No, Kasim.* You just *think* you are—because I'm the only girl who's ever given you attention.

We're friends, and you mistook that for love.

But we're just friends.

This isn't the 1950s, Kasim. Men and women *can* be just friends."

Kasim clenched his jaw. "*Friends.* Right."

"Look," Ruhi continued, "you're my best friend. But I want someone who—"

Kasim cut her off. "*Someone who isn't me.* Someone like *Imran.*"

"Don't drag him into this," Ruhi said. "This is about you and me. Kasim…Look. I want someone different, someone with ambition, a drive for life, someone with goals."

With a broken heart, Kasim slowly whispered, "An

ambitious person like *Imran*,"

Ruhi's cold voice echoed in Kasim's ears. "He's ambitious, knows what he wants, and regardless of what you think of him, he's a nice guy."

Kasim's voice breaks. "And I'm not *worthy* of your love!"

Ruhi's ice-cold demeanor was unrecognizable.

"Your delusion to think you love me."

Kasim inhaled sharply looking down shedding a single tear from his eye.

"Delusion?"

Ruhi didn't hesitate.

"*Yes*.

Kasim, what do you even *have* to offer?

You have no ambition, no drive, no goals.

You've had *everything* handed to you your entire life.

You have no desire for anything, you're average-looking, and you're *still* finishing your education. Still figuring your life out.

You're *still* living off your parents. You have nothing of yours!

Even if a man isn't good-looking, a woman wants someone she can *rely* on.

Not someone who's *lost.*

I need a man who can take charge.

I want more from life, Kasim, and from the person I want to be with,"

Kasim's throat tightened.

"Wow. Just say it, Ruhi…. you *want* to be with Imran."

"Leave him out of it!" she snapped. "*This is about you!* You need to wake up and realize we were *never* meant to be more than friends. You're *nice guy*, Kasim.

You'll make some girl really happy one day.

But that girl isn't me."

Kasim took a step toward her, his eyes glistening.

"You're *rejecting me for a man who will never see the real you. He'll never understand you.*

But I do."

Ruhi swallowed hard.

"I'm happy with who I am, Ruhi," Kasim continued.

"I don't have to pretend. But you...? You're becoming someone you're not.

I'm happy being myself; I'm happy in *my* world. And remember one thing: I may be a lot of things, but I'm not fake,"

Ruhi's breath caught. "Kasim—"

Kasim's voice dropped to a whisper.

"You're flying too high. One day, you'll fall *hard*... and I won't be there to catch you."

The finality in his voice made her chest tighten. Without another word, he turned and walked away. Ruhi stood frozen, watching his retreating figure disappear into the night.

And just like that, she *lost* her best friend.

***

ACT TWO

Seven years had passed since that fateful night in Lahore—the night Ruhi left everything behind and set off for Karachi to carve her own path in the fashion world. In just a few years, she had risen to become one of the most sought-after designers in the country, her name synonymous with elegance and innovation.

Yet, despite her meteoric success, loneliness had become a constant companion in the dazzling yet isolating world of glamour and entertainment. The only solace she found was in the unwavering presence of her cousin and closest friend, Saira.

Ruhi had deliberately severed ties with her past, keeping only sporadic contact with her family and completely keeping her distance from her college friends, especially Kasim. Reaching out to him had crossed her mind many times, but the weight of their last conversation—the sting of his parting words—held her back.

Kasim, it seemed, had vanished.

There were no traces of him on social media or casual mentions of his life in passing conversations. Her parents never mentioned him once. The ongoing feud between their families made any inquiries about him nearly impossible. It was as if he had disappeared into the shadows, leaving Ruhi with unanswered questions.

Then, an unexpected opportunity arose—an invitation to showcase her designs at the country's most prestigious celebrity fashion show. It was a career-defining moment.

But there was one catch—the event was in Lahore.

The city that held both the promise of her biggest professional breakthrough and the ghosts of a past she had long buried. Without hesitation, Ruhi accepted. This was her chance to step onto the global stage to solidify her legacy. But deep down, she knew returning to Lahore meant confronting the remnants of history she had tried to leave behind—especially the unresolved emotions tethered to Kasim.

The drive from the airport was filled with warmth and nostalgia. Omar and Kiran were delighted to have Ruhi and Saira back, and despite her excitement, Ruhi couldn't shake the subtle apprehension bubbling beneath the surface.

As they settled into the ride, Omar shared how Ruhi's supposed one-year internship had unexpectedly turned into an extended residency due to her rapid rise in the fashion industry. Though her family had visited her in Karachi, her absence had been deeply felt in Lahore.

Ruhi, unwilling to dwell on sentimentality, chuckled. *"Not everyone missed me, Abu. Let's not exaggerate."* She swiftly shifted the conversation to her father's work.

Omar revealed that he had retired from the hospital but

remained a board member, ensuring continued influence in the medical field. He spoke highly of a newly appointed doctor, describing them as one of the finest he had ever seen—respected among peers and admired for their dedication.

As they drove through familiar streets, Ruhi observed how much had changed, yet how much had remained the same. The city was evolving, but she knew the petty bickering between her father and Rehan Chaudhry would not. It was strangely comforting.

However, instead of heading straight home, Ruhi made a different decision that caught her parents off guard.

As the driver stops outside their house, she quickly steps out and heads straight to Chaudhry's residence. Omar and Kiran exchanged glances but said nothing, recognizing the quiet determination in their daughter's eyes.

Ruhi stepped inside the Chaudhry household and was immediately enveloped in warmth.

Rehan and Reshma's faces lit up as they welcomed her with open arms, showering her with love and admiration. Reshma admired Ruhi's new look and humility in coming and seeing them first.

"Regardless of the daily fights, you'll always be my second family."

Daniyal and Mahirah joined them, congratulating her on her success, and the atmosphere turned joyous, filled with laughter and nostalgia. Yet, amidst the heartfelt reunion, Ruhi's eyes discreetly scanned the house. Everything looked the same—the furniture, the decor, the warmth. Except for one glaring absence.

Kasim.

No one mentioned him. *Not once.* His name lingered on the edge of the conversation, carefully avoided as if uttering it would summon something painful. Ruhi didn't ask, and they didn't offer.

After bidding them farewell, she stepped outside. As she walked next door to her home, Ruhi glanced at the closed window of Kasim's room—the window where they had once shared countless silent conversations across their balconies.

A pang of guilt tightened in her chest. She had left so much unsaid that night. She had never imagined that would be their last conversation.

Inside the Chaudhry home, Reshma sat quietly in her room, applying lotion to her hands, lost in thought. Rehan entered, his expression softer than usual.

"She's done well for herself," he said, referring to Ruhi. His voice carried a rare note of admiration.

Reshma nodded but said nothing.

After a pause, Rehan exhaled. "We need to do something about Kasim. He's not the same, Reshma."

Reshma's hands stilled. She knew where this was going.

"It's time," Rehan continued. "He needs to get married. Maybe a wife will bring back the happiness he's lost."

Reshma sighed. "He won't even discuss it. The moment we bring it up, he shuts down or walks away."

Rehan ran a hand through his hair. "I lost my son somewhere along the way."

It wasn't an exaggeration. Seven years ago, Kasim was still Kasim. He still laughed and spent time with the family. But slowly, he withdrew. He buried himself in his work, locked himself in his room for hours, and distanced himself from everything and everyone.

It was as if a part of him had vanished—and they questioned what had changed but never knew exactly what had happened. His behavior change was a mystery to all.

"I think it's time we start looking," Rehan said.

Reshma hesitated. She had considered potential matches before, but deep in her heart, she knew there was only one girl for Kasim—and she was currently back in Lahore.

Ruhi.

She didn't say it aloud, but Rehan saw it in her eyes. He smiled at the thought. But the smile quickly faded.

"That's a dream we can't afford," he murmured.

And as he left the room, the weight of his sister's death settled over him like a shadow—one that, no matter how much time passed, refused to fade.

Ruhi stood near the window in her old bedroom, staring at the city she once called home. She should be focused on the fashion show. She should be preparing for her biggest moment yet. But all she could think about was him.

Kasim.

Where was he?

And if she saw him again, after all these years…

What would she even say?

Ruhi woke early the next morning, stepping onto her balcony with the quiet anticipation of watching the sunrise. It had become second nature—a habit from the past.

But for the first time in years, Kasim didn't emerge. Her eyes flickered toward his window. She saw movement inside his room, a shadow shifting behind the curtains, but the balcony door remained closed. A flicker of irritation burned within her.

Why did she care?

After all, it was he who had walked away first; he had chosen this distance. Before Ruhi could think further, the distant sound of a car engine caught her attention. She turned just in time to see a vehicle leaving the driveway, but the tinted windows concealed its occupants.

Ruhi clenched her jaw, frustrated for reasons she couldn't explain. Shaking off the unexpected emotion, she retreated inside. She had a long day ahead—no time to dwell on things that no longer mattered.

Ruhi had thrown herself back into work mode by the time she arrived at her studio. She met with her staff, distributors, and fellow designers, her energy sharp and commanding.

"The celebrity fashion show is our biggest platform yet," she told them, her voice steady with determination. "I expect nothing less than perfection."

The meeting was intense, packed with details about collections, sponsorships, and last-minute adjustments. Then, in the middle of the chaos, Imran appeared. Her former friend-turned-occasional-colleague strolled in with his usual arrogance, flashing an easy smile.

"Missed me?" he teased.

Ruhi barely glanced at him. "I'm busy. We'll talk later."

Imran's smirk faltered. "I've been trying to reach you for weeks, Ruhi. I even left messages with Saira."

At that moment, Saira, standing nearby, scoffed.

"No, you didn't."

Ruhi, absorbed in her work, barely registered their exchange. She engaged in her meeting with the sponsors and chairmen of the fashion show. Her meeting was cut short as she discovered Saira furiously yelling at Imran.

Ruhi frowned. "What's going on?"

Saira hesitated, clearly furious but unwilling to share details.

Ruhi turned to Imran. "Why have you been dodging me?"

His expression shifted, softening into an apology.

"Ruhi, come on. We've both been busy. Let's not do this." His voice was smooth, persuasive. Manipulative.

Against her better judgment, Ruhi let it go.

Ruhi calmed herself down to engage in a civil conversation. "You know why I've been trying to contact you?"

Imran brushed his hand against her face as she pushed it away abruptly. "Because you missed me."

Ruhi smirked.

"No because of the fashion show...Maybe instead of throwing yourself into glamor parties, you should focus on work."

Imran understood her tone, she meant business.

"Come on Ruhi, I was away—"

Saira interjected. "You should have stayed away."

Ruhi grew frustrated. "Okay, that's enough. Imran this is a one-of-a-kind fashion show; I need everyone's hundred percent.

As this is a celebrity fashion show the sponsors have chosen a celebrity couple as the showstopper."

"What?" Imran yelled.

Saira steps in as she knows Imran inner nature to childish tantrums.

"No need to raise your voice, Imran."

His charm faltered. His eyes darkened.

"Imran Ali and I'm *not* included."

Ruhi knew Imran had a celebrity complex, as he desired to be loved and acknowledged especially now as his celebrity status is threatened by a newcomer.

Ruhi explained as best as she could. "I never said that. You won't be the showstopper. But you still can be in the show."

He looked down his eyes filled with rage but still, he kept his composure, though barely. Instead, he turned to Ruhi with a proposition.

"Speak to the sponsors," he suggested smoothly. "Get them to replace the couple with me and another actress."

Ruhi shook her head. "That's not how this works, Imran."

Saira sighed as muttered rolling her eyes. *"Oh my god."*

He ignored her protest.

"You owe me, Ruhi. I helped build your public image. My presence will only elevate your brand.

Besides, remember our agreement for joint media appearances?"

Ruhi hesitated.

He saw his opening.

"This will help you, too. I can get you the costume designer for my international films."

The pressure was overwhelming. Her instincts screamed no, but she knew how the industry worked.

Publicity was everything.

Connections mattered.

Reluctantly, she agreed. "I try but I can't promise you anything. The final decision is the sponsors."

Saira, watching from the sidelines, was furious. Saira's phone began to buzz leading to a smile on her face. The atmosphere in the studio remained tense, and the topic of Kasim surfaced. Saira, casually watching one of his funny videos, giggled.

"God, I forgot how hilarious Kasim can be."

Ruhi shot her a sharp glare.

Saira smirked, unfazed. "What? It's good content."

Imran, never one to miss a chance to belittle someone, scoffed.

"Kasim? You still talk to that loser."

Saira's playful expression vanished. Her eyes darkened as she turned to Imran.

"Not everyone is defined by fame and money," she shot back. "At least he has morals."

Ruhi, sensing the brewing argument, quickly intervened.

"*Enough.*

Both of you—focus on your work."

Imran rolled his eyes but didn't argue. He had more important things to focus on—like getting what he wanted. Saira and Ruhi returned to work. Ruhi's mind focused on her duties, but her subconscious wished to understand why Saira kept in touch with Kasim.

Later that night, Omar joined Ruhi as she worked in the living room. His tone was casual, but his question wasn't.

"So, Ruhi," he began, "have you given any thought to marriage?"

Ruhi sighed. "Not now, Abu. My career is my focus."

Omar smiled knowingly.

"I understand. But I do want to introduce you to someone— his name is Irfan. He's—"

"Abu, please." Ruhi shook her head. "I'm *not* interested."

Omar didn't press further. Instead, his phone rang. Ruhi noticed his entire demeanor change. He answered, and his face lit up with warmth.

"Ah, Kasim—how you doing?"

Ruhi's breath hitched.

Kasim?

Her father's warm laughter and genuine gratitude toward Kasim left her stunned.

What was Kasim doing calling her father?

When Omar hung up, he turned to Ruhi. "Think about what I said," he advised before leaving the room.

Ruhi sat there, mind racing.

Why was Kasim calling her father?

What had she missed over these seven years?

These questioned lingered in her mind giving her a restless sleep. The next day at the studio, Ruhi delivered the final verdict to Imran.

"The sponsors aren't agreeing. They won't replace the showstoppers. If we push too hard, we'll risk losing funding altogether."

Imran's expression hardened. His jaw clenched. His rage simmered beneath the surface, but he forced himself to stay calm.

"Fine," he said after a beat.

"I understand."

But Ruhi knew better. There was something off about his tone.

Something dangerous.

Before he left, he turned back to her, his lips curling into a slow, knowing smile.

"I'll see you tonight," he murmured.

The words sounded more like a warning than a promise. Ruhi couldn't shake the uneasy feeling settling in her chest as Imran walked away. Something told her that Imran wasn't done yet. And whatever he was planning—it wouldn't be good.

Ruhi and Saira remained deeply engrossed in their preparations as the day progressed, unaware of the danger lurking within the studio. Ruhi had a dreadful feeling the whole day. Unable to shake it off, she told herself it was her nerves.

Imran returns from his TV shoot as he watches from the shadows, moved with calculated precision. With everyone absorbed in their tasks, he reached into his coat pocket and retrieved a small bottle of oil. Glancing around to ensure no one was watching, he discreetly poured the liquid onto the runway stage.

The trap was set.

Moments later, he approached Ruhi, feigning interest in learning the precise runway walk.

"Show me how it's done, Ruhi," he said smoothly, his eyes gleaming with something sinister.

Ruhi, already exhausted but ever the professional, sighed.

"Fine. Follow my lead."

As she took her first step onto the stage, her foot *slipped*. Ruhi let out a sharp gasp as her ankle twisted violently beneath her weight, and before she could steady herself, she collapsed onto the floor.

A piercing cry of pain erupted from her lips as the entire studio erupted into chaos. The sound of her fall echoed through the auditorium.

Saira sprinted to her side.

"Ruhi! Are you okay?"

Ruhi clutched her ankle, her face contorted in pain. Her vision blurred as panic and agony intertwined.

Imran smirked as he held Ruhi's hand.

"Get her in the car," Saira commanded, taking control of the situation.

As the staff scrambled to help, Saira grabbed her phone and urgently called Ruhi's family.

"There has been an accident. Meet us at the hospital."

Saira has a staff member drive their car to the hospital. Imran insisted he'd meet them at the hospital.

As he entered his car, he told his driver to *"take me home"* as he threw the oil bottle out of the window as the cars drove opposite directions.

Ruhi arrives at the hospital and is rushed straight into a room. A kind nurse arrives and assesses her injuries. She informed her that a senior doctor would be in shortly.

The tension in the hospital room was suffocating as Ruhi waited for the doctor. Her thoughts swirled between pain, frustration, and confusion. Then, the nurse returned, a polite smile on her face.

"The doctor will be with you shortly. Dr. Kasim Chaudhry will be treating you."

Ruhi's heart stopped. Her breath caught in her throat.

No. That's not possible.

Before she could react, the door swung open. And there he was.

Kasim.

But not the Kasim she remembered.

The man who walked in was not the boy she once knew. Gone was the hesitant, uncertain young man from her past. He walked in with conviction.

This Kasim was different—broader, taller, confident. No longer stout and unkept but handsome. His muscular build caught Ruhi's attention, but she maintained to keep her careless demeanor.

Her occasional glance showed her he wore a sleek grey suit, his sharp features framed by a neatly trimmed beard. His presence was commanding and effortlessly authoritative.

Ruhi's mouth went dry.

Saira, unable to hide her excitement, greeted him warmly.

"Wow, Kasim. Look at you."

Kasim gave her a brief nod and a polite smile—but he didn't spare Ruhi a single glance. The air was thick with unspoken words. The nurse began explaining Ruhi's injury, detailing the necessary steps for recovery.

Kasim listened, arms crossed, nodding occasionally. Then, without a word to Ruhi, he placed a reassuring hand on

Saira's shoulder as he turned to leave.

And just like that, he was gone.

Ruhi sat there, her chest tightening in a mixture of shock, confusion, and—for the first time in years—anger. Her parents arrived soon after, and their concern was evident. The nurse explained that the physician was in the process of evaluating the injury and that Ruhi would require an X-ray before determining the severity of the injury.

Her thoughts were in turmoil as Ruhi was wheeled into the radiology department. Kasim had changed not just in appearance but in demeanor and presence.

He didn't even acknowledge her.

Not a *single* word.

Not even a glance.

The realization stung far more than her injured ankle.

Back in the hospital room, Ruhi's parents continued to fuss over her.

"You need complete bed rest," her mother insisted.

Ruhi shook her head stubbornly.

"I'll work from home if I have to. I'm *not* abandoning the fashion show."

Their argument was still ongoing when Kasim reentered the room. His presence immediately shifted the atmosphere. He greeted her parents with warmth and familiarity.

"There's no need to worry," he reassured them. "It's just a sprain. She'll need a splint for two weeks."

But Omar, ever the protective father, wasn't satisfied.

"I want the best care for my daughter," he stated firmly.

Kasim, remaining professional, nodded. "If you'd prefer, another doctor can oversee her physical therapy. She'll need about three months of rehab."

Omar shook his head. "No. I want *you* to take care of her."

Ruhi's eyes widened.

Her father trusted Kasim that much?

75

Omar continued proudly.

"I've followed your achievements, Kasim. I know you graduated top of your class. There's *no one* I trust more with my daughter's recovery."

Kasim hesitated. His expression was unreadable. Then, finally, he agreed. Ruhi exhaled, stunned.

He had barely looked at her.

Barely spoken to her.

Yet, he was going to be the one helping her recover?

The thought sent a strange shiver through her.

Kasim informs the nurse.

"Go ahead and prepare a splint. I'll bandage and place it myself."

He exited without a word, angering Ruhi further.

Kiran kissed her daughter's forehead. "You must be hungry. We'll grab some food."

Neither spoke.

The weight of the past pressed down on them.

Then—the door opened.

Ruhi's parents entered, unaware of the moment they had interrupted, as she quickly released his hand.

Kasim immediately stepped away, regaining his composure. He exchanged pleasantries with them before walking out, his expression unreadable. Exiting the hospital room, he spotted his parents waiting in the lobby.

His brows furrowed.

"What are you doing here?" he asked.

Rehan and Reshma, genuinely surprised, exchanged glances.

"We have a doctor's appointment," his mother answered.

"In this wing?" Kasim asked again.

"The nurse told us she'll come and get us from here when the doctor is available," Rehan said, maintaining his cover story.

Kasim nodded slowly as Omar and Kiran entered the hallway.

"Kasim. Thank you for coming on short notice." Omar said, shaking his hand.

"My pleasure. Not to worry, she'll recover quickly." Kasim said as he bid them farewell.

Omar and Kiran, passing by, noticed Rehan and Reshma and left with pleased smiles.

Inside the hospital room, another reunion was about to unfold. Rehan and Reshma, seizing the opportunity, rushed into Ruhi's room.

Their best friend's daughter was like a daughter to them—the girl they had always loved—was finally back home. But so much had changed.

And neither Ruhi nor Kasim could predict what's yet to come.

***

After Ruhi was discharged, the familiar walls of her home provided little comfort. Her family accommodated her as best as they could, but her mind stayed at the hospital, rerunning the events of the day. She tried to brush her feelings away but kept searching for an answer.

Why do I feel this way?

The night was long, and her thoughts refused to settle. Kasim's presence had shattered something inside her—something she thought had been buried in the past.

The man she had seen at the hospital wasn't the Kasim she remembered.

He was different now.

Confident, composed, and distant.

Too distant.

Ruhi's mind replayed their silent moments—his unwavering professionalism, the way he hadn't looked at her until it was absolutely necessary. The way he had ignored their history. She tossed and turned, restless, before finally giving up.

Sitting up, she glanced at Saira, who was fast asleep beside her.

"Saira," Ruhi whispered, nudging her.

Saira groaned, pulling the blanket over her head.

"Go to sleep, Ruhi."

Ruhi sighed, knowing her cousin wouldn't entertain her late-night spirals. But she couldn't suppress the pull—the need to see for herself. She thought.

Why do I care?

Hell with him.

He's just my doctor, nothing more.

Her feelings took control of her mind.

But he was my best friend...

I just don't understand...

Why is he behaving this way?

Grabbing her crutches, Ruhi slowly made her way onto the balcony.

The cold air stung her skin as she stepped forward, gazing across the familiar space that once connected her and Kasim.

His curtains were closed, but his lights were on.

A small sign that he was still awake. She quickly grabs a pebble and throws it at the window…

No response.

She stood there for a long moment, her heart heavy.

The last time they had stood face to face, it had ended in anger, heartbreak, and finality.

"You're flying too high. One day, you'll fall hard, and I won't be there to catch you."

His voice echoed in her ears.

Ruhi winced at the memory, gripping the balcony railing as emotions surged. Kasim had once been her best friend. The one who had understood her better than anyone else. And yet, in the seven years she had been away, he had never once reached out.

Her thoughts spiral as she glared at his window.

Never once did he ask how I was.

If I'm happy.

If I missed him.

Was it that easy to let me go?

Have I let him go?

With a tired sigh, Ruhi turned away and retreated inside, her heart a tangled mess of emotions. Lying back down, she forced herself to think rationally.

Yes, Kasim had changed.

Yes, it unsettled her. But hadn't she moved on, too?

Hadn't she built a life without him?

She had everything she ever dreamed of—success, recognition, independence.

Yet, why does it feel like something is missing?

Despite herself, she felt proud of Kasim. He had become someone important. He had worked hard and made a name for himself.

And yet—he had never tried to find her. He was the one who had distanced himself all these years. And if that was the case, then maybe it was time to accept the truth.

Maybe their connection, once so strong, so undeniable, had finally shattered beyond repair.

Maybe it was better that way.

With that thought, she closed her eyes, forcing herself to let go.

She would not reach out.

And she would not look back.

Dastaan -e- Ishq

The morning air was crisp as Kasim adjusted his coat, preparing to leave for the hospital. His demeanor was the same as he was in the hospital. He thought to himself.

Ruhi was just another patient; his past wouldn't reflect his treatment plan. As he reached for his keys, his mother, Reshma, intercepted him. She held out a small container of soup.

"Take this to Ruhi," she said softly, her voice carrying the same warmth for the girl who once felt like a daughter to her.

Kasim hesitated for a fraction of a second.

"*Ma,* she—"

"Just take it, Kasim."

There was no room for refusal. With a quiet sigh, Kasim nodded, taking the container before heading out. As he stepped out of the door, he heard his name called.

"Kasim."

He quickly turned around to find Mahirah and Daniyal.

Daniyal quickly caught up with him as his wife followed. "We'll join you."

"You should be resting," Kasim told Mahirah.

"I will, but walking is good for me. Plus, we're just going next door." Mahirah said they headed to Omar's house.

The trio entered Omar's house and was greeted by Kiran, who was thrilled to have them over. She quickly called Omar down.

"We have something to tell you," Daniyal said in excitement.

"We couldn't wait." Mahirah grabbed Kiran's hand and placed it on her belly.

Mahirah was pregnant.

"NO! Seriously," Kiran said, wiping her tears of joy.

"I'm so happy for you; after all these years, god has heard our prayers," Omar said, hugging Daniyal.

Mahirah and Daniyal were met with joyous laughter and

heartfelt congratulations.

The news spread warmth through the family, filling the home with excitement. Daniyal, overwhelmed with happiness.

"There is something we both wanted to ask you." Daniyal said hold Mahirah's hand.

"Anything for you, son," Omar responded.

"We want you and your family to come to the baby shower," Mahirah said as Omar and Kiran glanced at each other uncomfortably.

"We're not taking *no* for an answer," Kasim said as Ruhi entered on her clutches.

Kasim did not acknowledge her presence as he quickly left to go into the living room.

"Glad you're here," Mahirah said as she whispered in her ear, she's pregnant.

"No. Seriously. I'm so happy for you." Ruhi said, hugging her.

"Daniyal, look, you're like my son, but you know the situation between me and your father. I don't—" Omar said calmly.

"I'll handle Abba." Daniyal responded.

"We don't want to spoil—" Kiran interjected.

Daniyal wrapped his arm around Omar.

"You've been part of my life since I was born. *You* brought me home. And for me, you'll *always* be family.

Abba knows that, and if anything, I'll deal with him if he says anything."

Kiran sighed. "I hope you know what you're doing."

Mahirah firmly stated. "We do."

Omar hesitated but finally gave a reluctant nod.

"For Mahirah, *I will*."

Soon after, Daniyal, Mahirah, Omar, and his wife left to visit someone at the hospital, bidding their farewell to Ruhi, who made her way to the living room.

At last, she was alone with Kasim. The tension was immediate. Kasim sat on the couch, focused on adjusting his medical equipment.

He didn't look at Ruhi.

Didn't acknowledge her presence.

Their awkward science was interrupted by Saira's arrival. Kasim smiled at Saira when she entered, engaging in light conversation.

Ruhi stiffened.

A strange, unexpected annoyance flared inside her at his smile.

Why did it bother her?

She quickly masked her emotions, handing Saira a list of tasks.

"You should get back to the studio," she instructed.

Saira, oblivious to Ruhi's irritation, nodded and left. And then, there was silence. A thick, heavy silence filled the air between them. Ruhi, determined not to let it get to her, folded her arms and leaned back. Then, unable to resist the urge, she spoke—her tone sharp, condescending.

"So, Dr. Chaudhry, how much longer until I can walk without these crutches?"

Kasim's jaw tensed at her deliberate use of his title. His response was calm but detached.

"A month. Three sessions a week for therapy."

Ruhi pursed her lips, choosing not to respond further.

Without another word, Kasim moved toward her. He crouched down gracefully on the floor, his movements fluidly controlled.

Before Ruhi could question him, he gently removed the splint from her ankle. She eased into her chair as his fingers pressed against her skin, an electrifying sensation. He massaged the sore muscles with a practiced ease.

A wave of relief washed over her. She didn't want to admit it—but it felt good.

Neither of them spoke.

Kasim remained focused, silent. The warmth of his hands, the unexpected gentleness, sent a strange shiver through Ruhi. Then, after a moment, he set her foot down.

"Does it hurt?" he asked.

Ruhi, unwilling to let herself feel anything, snapped back, *"No."*

His expression remained unreadable. He handed Ruhi a small therapy ball.

"Roll your foot on this—gently," he instructed.

Ruhi, still irritated, pressed down on the ball too forcefully. A sharp pain shot up her ankle. She let out a small cry before instinctively grabbing his arm. Her fingernails dug into his skin, leaving faint red marks.

Kasim didn't flinch. Didn't react at all. Only when she realized what she had done did Ruhi soften, her voice barely above a whisper.

"I— I'm sorry."

Kasim's response was quite calm.

"I've been through worse."

His words lingered in the air, carrying a weight Ruhi couldn't quite grasp. Shifting away from the moment, Kasim returned to his clinical tone.

"Don't put weight on your ankle for the next few days. Use the crutches."

He handed her a sheet of exercises.

"Do these twice a day. We'll continue therapy tomorrow."

Ruhi nodded, still feeling the ghost of his touch on her skin. As Kasim gathered his belongings, he turned to leave. Then, with his back still to her, he spoke—his voice lower, almost reluctant.

"*Ma* sent soup for you. Make sure you drink it."

Without waiting for a response, he walked out. Ruhi sat there, staring after him.

Conflicted.

Frustrated.

And, for reasons she refused to acknowledge—aching.

Throughout the day, Ruhi's mind was restless. No matter how much she tried to focus on the upcoming fashion show, one thought kept creeping back in—Kasim.

His demeanor.

His voice.

His distance.

This wasn't the Kasim she had known. There was a sternness in his tone, a quiet authority that hadn't been there before. He had always been reserved but never cold. The way he barely acknowledged her, the way he refused to meet her eyes for too long—it unsettled her.

Was he angry?

Had he truly let go of their past?

Did he no longer care at all?

The thought left an uncomfortable weight on her chest. She

shook it off.

"I'm overthinking. We just need time to adjust. Things will go back to normal."

Or at least, she hoped they would. Pushing aside the confusion, Ruhi forced herself back into work mode, throwing herself into the final preparations for the show. But no matter how busy she kept herself, Kasim lingered in the back of her mind.

That night, after another restless evening, Ruhi climbed out of bed to fetch a glass of water. The house was quiet, and everyone was fast asleep.

She made her way to the kitchen carefully, balancing on her crutches, refusing to wake anyone for help. But as she reached for the glass—She lost her balance.

The world tilted.

A sharp cry escaped Ruhi's lips as she tumbled, landing hard on the cold marble floor. The crash shattered the silence of the house. Within moments, her father rushed into the room, followed closely by Saira and her mother.

"Ruhi!" her father exclaimed, kneeling beside her.

"Are you hurt?"

She winced as she tried to sit up, pain shooting through her ankle. Her father examined her carefully, his medical expertise taking over.

"I don't think you've worsened the sprain," he said after a moment, "but you need to be careful. Maybe I should call Kasim to check on you."

Ruhi stiffened.

"No," she said quickly.

Her father frowned. "Ruhi—"

"I'm fine, Abu. Kasim will be here in the morning for my scheduled therapy. There's no need to disturb him now."

Her father didn't look convinced but eventually relented with a nod.

"Fine. But you need to take it easy."

Saira helped Ruhi back to bed, adjusting the pillows for

support. As she pulled the blanket over her, Saira sighed.

"You should've just asked me for water."

Ruhi exhaled, feeling both frustrated and embarrassed.

"Don't tell Kasim about this," she muttered.

Saira gave her a knowing smirk.

"Why? Afraid he'll scold you like a real doctor?"

Ruhi didn't answer.

Because deep down, she knew the real reason. She didn't want Kasim to see her like this—weak, vulnerable. Not when she was still trying to figure him out. Not when she wasn't sure where they stood.

**

The morning sun streamed through the curtains as Ruhi sat in the living room, weighed down by the events of the night and the demands of her work. Stress piled on, making it increasingly difficult to face Kasim.

Ruhi understood the significance of her fashion show, yet even with Saira's help, she worried things might not come together. Her thoughts drifted between work and Kasim, bracing herself for his inevitable cold demeanor as she slowly settled into her emotions.

Ruhi, lost in her thoughts, didn't realize Kasim had entered the house carrying his medical equipment. She saw this as an opportunity and called Imran. Kasim continued setting up his medical equipment as Ruhi, engaged in a Zoom call, barely spared him a glance.

"Imran, I assure you, I'm fine," she said smoothly, her voice professional yet distant.

She thanked him for being a good friend and stealing a glance at Kasim. But Kasim remained indifferent and focused on setting up his equipment. Not a flicker of reaction.

Ruhi pressed on.

"How about lunch or dinner to discuss the lineup?" she offered.

Imran readily agreed. Her gaze flicked toward Kasim again, but he didn't flinch. Not even a hint of jealousy, irritation—nothing.

Not that she cared, Ruhi told herself.

She excused herself from the call.

"Wait, let me say hi to your doctor and thank him—" Imran started, but Ruhi quickly cut the call as Saira entered, and Kasim quickly welcomed her.

Ruhi knew it was best to not let Imran know that Kasim was her physician. She quickly glanced at Kasim, who didn't acknowledge her phone call. Instead, he returned with Saira to the kitchen. Ruhi masked her emotions, but something about this irritated her.

Before leaving, Saira casually mentioned, "I'll meet you for lunch later, Kasim."

He nodded in acknowledgment, and Ruhi felt her irritation deepen.

"How long will today's session take? I have work to do," Ruhi asked curtly.

Kasim ignored her.

Annoyed, she repeated the question, her tone sharper this time.

"How long will this take?"

"It'll take an hour," he replied coldly. "And there's no need to take your work frustration out on me."

Ruhi's jaw tightened. She said nothing as he moved in front of her, kneeling down to begin therapy.

Without a word, he grabbed her foot. The electrifying sensation returned from his touch as the sun glistened on his face. But she knew not to cave in; she simply ignored his touch by slightly moving her foot.

"I told you to lay off your feet."

"I did," she lied.

Kasim didn't buy it.

"You fell, didn't you?" His voice was firm, unreadable.

"It was nothing," Ruhi dismissed. "A minor fall."

"Congratulations," Kasim said flatly. "Your *minor fall* caused a *minor* fracture, which means your recovery time just doubled."

Ruhi froze.

He called for the housemaid to bring warm water while he began massaging her ankle. The pressure of his hands sent an uninvited warmth through her. She shifted uncomfortably. But he didn't stop. She tried pulling away, but his grip remained firm.

The maid arrived, setting down the warm water. Kasim gently placed her foot inside.

"There's no need for you to become superwoman," he said, his tone bordering on mocking. "You need to rest."

Ruhi, agitated, yanked her foot out angrily.

Kasim's gaze hardened.

"What is your issue?"

Ruhi responded with irritation. "I think I need another doctor."

Kasim's expression remained neutral, but something in his posture stiffened.

"Gladly," he said. "I didn't want to be here anyway. Your father asked me, and I made him a promise. That's the only reason I'm here."

Ruhi folded her arms. "I'll talk to my Abu. He'll understand. You don't need to come since you clearly don't *want* to."

Kasim began packing his medical bag without a word. Just as he was about to leave, Omar entered.

"What's going on?" Omar asked, sensing the thick tension in the air.

"I think it's best that your daughter gets another doctor,"

Kasim stated simply. "At her request."

Omar's brows furrowed.

"No," he said firmly. "I only want the best doctor for her—and that's *you.*"

"Abu, he doesn't even want to be here," Ruhi argued.

Omar crossed his arms. "That's not the point. For your well-being, I asked Kasim because he *is* the best."

Ruhi rolled her eyes. "There are other doctors in this city,"

Omar's voice hardened. "Not as good as him. If another doctor takes over, your recovery will take twice as long. I've made my decision."

Ruhi gritted her teeth. There was no point in fighting it. Kasim, unbothered, scribbled on a prescription pad.

"I'll write an injection for nighttime. It's a painkiller," Kasim said.

"You'll need to give it to her," Omar instructed. "I'll be at a wedding and won't return for a few days."

"Abu, please—" Ruhi responded as Omar raised her hand to quiet her down.

Kasim nodded. "If she falls again, it'll worsen her condition; please call me immediately."

Omar gave Ruhi a pointed look. "This is for your own good." Then, he left the room.

The second the door closed, Kasim turned to Ruhi. Without a word, he grabbed her foot again, placing it back into the water. She looked away. He kneeled beside the tub, his hands submerged as he massaged her feet. The silence was deafening.

Kasim's phone rang.

"Yeah. I'll be there soon. Everything's set? Good. I'll be there in 30 minutes."

He hung up, standing up as if nothing had happened.

Ruhi exhaled.

"If you want, I'll convince him," Kasim offered.

She raised an eyebrow. "What, are you afraid of a challenge?"

Kasim's jaw tensed.

Then, in a low voice, he asked, "I'm going to ask you one last time—what's your problem?"

Ruhi's gaze locked onto his.

"You're my problem," she admitted, voice laced with anger, hurt, and frustration.

Kasim's eyes darkened.

"You walk in here like we're strangers. Like you don't even know me."

"I don't know *this* version of you," Kasim shot back.

Ruhi's chest tightened.

"I could say the same about you."

Kasim crossed his arms.

"You know. Your problem has always been that *you* want

things *your* way.

So why is it bothering you now after all these years?"

"Because you cut me off completely."

Kasim scoffed.

"Because you wanted me to."

"I *never* wanted to end our friendship," Ruhi argued. "You decided for us."

Kasim let out a humorless chuckle.

"I'm not the one who packed up everything and moved to Karachi without a word."

Ruhi swallowed.

"You never even told me you wanted to study medicine."

Kasim's face darkened.

"Because, as a friend, you never cared about what *I* wanted," he said coldly. "Our friendship was mostly about your needs."

Ruhi felt the sting.

"I've always been there for you, Kasim."

He laughed—bitter, disbelieving.

"You'll never admit when you're wrong." He shook his head. "I don't even know why we're having this conversation. We're *not* even friends."

Ruhi's heart clenched.

"Clearly," she whispered.

Kasim grabbed his medicine bag and headed for the door without another word. He paused.

"I'll be back for your painkiller injection later," he said, voice impersonal, distant.

"In the meantime, I'll find you a replacement doctor." And then, he walked away.

Leaving Ruhi with a heart that ached in ways she couldn't understand.

***

The day carried on as usual, but the weight of her conversation with Kasim pressed heavily on her. She tried to lose herself in work, yet his words echoed relentlessly in her mind— *"We're not friends."*

If we're not friends, then what are we? she wondered.

How did we become enemies?

A deep sense of abandonment settled over her. She had never imagined that, after all these years, facing Kasim would be this painful. Saira returned home to find Ruhi sitting on the couch, arms crossed, mood sour.

"What's wrong with you?" Saira asked, plopping down beside her.

"It's nothing," Ruhi muttered.

Saira gave her a knowing look. "Only one person can get you in a mood like this."

Ruhi sighed. "Don't worry, it's nothing."

Saira wasn't buying it. "I don't think so. What did he do?"

Ruhi hesitated, admitting, "We had a stupid fight… years ago. Now he's saying things that aren't true."

"Like?"

"That I'm selfish. Our friendship was one-sided, and I never cared about what he was going through."

Saira's expression shifted.

"Unfortunately," she said carefully, "I agree with Kasim."

Ruhi's head snapped up. "What?"

"Look, no matter how angry you were back then, you should've at least said goodbye. And over the years, you could've tried to make amends. You two were childhood friends, Ruhi. He deserved that much."

Ruhi folded her arms. "How am I selfish?"

Saira sighed, choosing her words carefully.

"You let go of your friendship for a dream. You never looked back. And as for attention—Kasim's right."

Ruhi furrowed her brows. "What are you talking about?"

Saira exhaled.

"During your fashion show—the one that got you your big break—Kasim was struggling.

A lot.

He was about to be kicked out of college because his grades were slipping.

He was taking extra classes, pulling all-nighters, trying to stay afloat… and at the same time, he was helping you.

Without saying a word."

Ruhi's heart dropped.

"I— I didn't know," she whispered.

"I know," Saira said, standing up.

"But I thought you should know."

As she left, Ruhi sat silently, guilt pressing against her chest. She had never considered what Kasim had been going through. She had never asked. She never noticed his struggles.

He never mentioned or complained.

His selfless act became her guilt.

The realization weighed heavily on her. No matter how much she tried to distract herself, her reflection of the past haunted her.

Later that night, Ruhi was in bed, pretending to read a magazine, when a knock echoed at her door.

"Come in," she called.

Saira peeked in. "Kasim's here with the injection. If you need anything, I'll be downstairs."

Ruhi swallowed. "Okay."

A few minutes later, there was another knock.

"It's open," Ruhi said.

Kasim entered, carrying his medical bag.

Ruhi attempted to get out of bed, but her injury made it difficult.

"Stay in bed," Kasim instructed his voice firm yet patient.

He sat beside her, taking out the injection.

Ruhi's eyes widened.

Then—She screamed. And jumped onto the bed, standing on one leg. Hold on to the headboard for her dear life.

Kasim blinked. "What are you doing?"

"That needle is huge!" Ruhi shouted, pointing at it dramatically.

Kasim sighed. "It's nothing. Get down."

"I know you're doing this on purpose," she accused.

"I'm not. I'm just doing my job."

Ruhi crossed her arms. "Remember when we fell off our bikes as kids, and I refused to get the injection?"

Kasim smirked slightly. "Yeah. And you still got it. And it didn't hurt."

Ruhi, of course, ignored that part.

"I know *you're* enjoying this," she grumbled as she threw a pillow at him. "You're mad at me, and this is your revenge."

Kasim rolled his eyes. "You're acting crazy.

Get down, Ruhi."

"You know how much I hate injections! You're doing this on purpose."

"I'm not… You're making this worse."

Ruhi, still standing on one leg, wobbled—And lost her balance.

Kasim moved fast.

He grabbed her arm, pulling her toward him.

A slight breeze of fresh air touched their hearts. His arms wrapped around her waist as she leans on him. Her hair grazed his face like a whisper, sending a quiet tremor down his spine—a feeling unfamiliar, yet hauntingly sweet.

Their bodies were suddenly too close, their eyes locked.

Unable to look away.

Ruhi's breath hitched as her heart skipped a beat. This was new.

They couldn't look away.

The moment stretched, the air between them heavy.

Gently, Kasim guided her back onto the bed. Their eyes remained locked as—he quickly gave her the injection. He smiled for the first time.

"All done!" Kasim said softly.

Ruhi blinked.

"... I didn't even feel it," she admitted.

Kasim smirked. "Told you."

His touch lingered for just a second before he pulled away. He stood up to leave. But before he could—Ruhi grabbed his hand.

Kasim stilled.

Her fingers tightened around his wrist, refusing to let go.

He turned back slowly.

Ruhi sat up, closer than ever, looking at him with something he hadn't seen in years—genuine sadness.

"I'm so sorry, Kasim," she said, voice barely above a whisper.

He didn't move.

Didn't speak.

He did not expect this.

"I haven't been a good friend to you," she admitted, her eyes searching his. "You were right. About all of it."

Kasim's throat tightened. He wanted to leave. But his feet wouldn't move.

"I don't know how to get past what happened," Ruhi continued, voice shaking.

"But we're older now.

Wiser.

Maybe we can be friends again.

Maybe we can start over."

Kasim stared at her, speechless.

Ruhi's eyes shimmered.

"Even *god* gives second chances."

The walls he had built over the years—the bitterness, the resentment, the distance—cracked. For the first time in years, Kasim let himself feel.

He nodded slowly.

Then—Ruhi wrapped her arms around him. A single tear slipped from Kasim's eye as he closed his arms around her.

He smiled.

"I'll do everything in my power to make you recover faster," he whispered. Then, without another word, he walked away.

Leaving Ruhi, for the first time in years—

At peace.

DASTAAN -E- ISHQ

ACT THREE

At first, things were awkward. There were pauses where laughter used to be, guarded words where honesty once flowed freely. But slowly, they found their rhythm again. Ruhi made an effort to ask about Kasim's day, something she had never done before.

Kasim, in turn, asked about her time in Karachi—particularly her career. Since both of them were familiar with high-stress environments, he was curious about how she coped with the pressures of her work. In her response, she shared how she had learned—through trial and error—to maintain her calm, a hard-earned lesson that had shaped her.

He asked if the fashion industry had treated her well and what it was like working in the entertainment world. She replied with a measured "yes and no." Always outspoken, she had often been perceived as arrogant or cutthroat.

Sometimes, that boldness worked in her favor; other times, it cost her valuable opportunities. Over time, she learned the importance of her words and how to express them with intention and positivity.

Kasim noticed the remarkable growth in her. She was no longer the same Ruhi who once reacted with a tense, impulsive energy. Now, she carried herself with quiet composure, fully aware of her surroundings.

Ruhi, in turn, found these conversations with Kasim unexpectedly meaningful. No one had ever taken such an interest in her journey or personal growth. For the first time, she truly felt that she mattered—that her work mattered.

Over tea, they sat in the yard every evening, exchanging stories. The walls between them softened, piece by piece. For the first time in years, Ruhi felt light again. She felt free of her daily burdens. Kasim showed her the respect she truly deserved, by acknowledging her. Omar and Kiran were pleased to see her smiling, free from the stress that had consumed her.

And as for Kasim's family—they, too, noticed a shift. He was happier. More open. He spent time with his father and brother and even joked back at his father's usual criticisms—a sight that hadn't been seen in years.

Things were finally falling into place. As Ruhi's physical therapy intensified, she and Kasim spent even more time together. Kasim adjusted his schedule, increasing her sessions to two hours daily—determined to help her recover before the fashion show.

Ruhi, despite her family's protests, threw herself into work. Deadlines loomed, meetings piled up, and the pressure mounted. And Kasim, between his demanding hospital shifts, still spent every free moment with her—telling himself it was only for her recovery. He ignored the way his heart raced whenever she smiled at him.

The way he noticed every little thing about her. The way she looked at him differently now—like she was truly seeing him for the first time. But he pushed it all aside. He told himself.

"We're just friends." Things were finally normal.

Why make things complicated?

Ruhi's absence from work began to take a toll. Even with Saira picking up the slack, things were falling behind. Ruhi tried working from home, but it wasn't enough. She started calling her designers for in-house meetings, desperate to keep everything on track. The stress weighed on her heavily. But the only thing that seemed to ease it?

Spending time with Kasim.

Listening to his stories about medical school, his training, and the world he had built for himself in her absence. The way he spoke about his passion made her forget her own worries—if only for a little while.

One evening, Ruhi sat at her desk, overwhelmed. Papers scattered across the surface. Emails flooding in. Deadlines closing in. Kasim walked in, his medical bag in hand. He took one look at her and knew. She didn't say much. Didn't need to. Her exhaustion was written all over her face. Without a word, he moved all the files off her desk. Then, he closed her laptop.

Ruhi snapped her head up.

"Kasim—"

"Ruhi."

His voice was steady.

"Let's take a break."

"I don't have time for a break," she argued. "The show is in two weeks."

Kasim crossed his arms.

"And you won't make it to the show if you keep going like this,"

She exhaled sharply, running a hand through her hair. Kasim watched her, his expression softening.

"Get ready. Let's go," Kasim said, handing Ruhi a cane.

"I have a lot of work," she protested.

"Think of it as part of your therapy," Kasim replied, already helping her out of the house.

"Where are we going?" Ruhi asked as he opened the car door for her.

Kasim didn't answer, only offering a small smile as she entered. His family watched them leave from the front porch, exchanging suspicious glances.

They drove through familiar streets until the car slowed down near a park. As Kasim parked, Ruhi's eyes flickered toward a small street vendor nearby. The sight alone made her smile. She didn't even have to ask. Kasim knew. He always knew. The only thing that could instantly lift her mood.

Ice cream.

And not just any ice cream—this ice cream, from this vendor. The same one they had gone to since childhood.

"Two ice creams," Kasim said, placing the order.

The vendor handed them their cones, and they began to walk, eating in comfortable silence. Ruhi took a bite, savoring the familiar taste.

"You still remember that ice cream makes everything better?" she asked, glancing at him.

Kasim smiled, his eyes warm.

"Doesn't it?"

They walked a little further before Ruhi turned to him.

"So, Doctor Saab, you never told me you wanted to join medicine?"

Kasim shrugged.

"I knew I wanted to do something… it just took me longer to figure it out."

He looked at her.

"But *you*… You knew you wanted to be a fashion designer."

A gust of wind blew a few strands of Ruhi's hair over her face. Without thinking, Kasim reached over and gently

125

tucked them behind her ear. Ruhi's breath hitched, but she said nothing.

"I am very proud of you and your accomplishments," she said after a moment.

Kasim's gaze softened.

"As I'm proud of you. I've always admired your ambition."

Ruhi hesitated, then admitted, "You've built quite a life for yourself… but I've missed my friend. The one who was always around, who openly talked to me."

Kasim smirked.

"You could always knock. Though, throwing pebbles at my window is more your style."

Ruhi laughed.

"So, you *were* awake that night… and didn't come out?"

Kasim smiled knowingly but didn't answer. Ruhi glances at him, catching his eye on her.

"I'm proud you won the first female fashion award within a

126

year. *Impressive,*" Kasim remarked.

Ruhi's brows raised.

"How do you know that?"

Kasim gave a slight shrug.

"I know *more* than you think."

Ruhi narrowed her eyes.

"So… Dr. Saab, you've been keeping tabs on *me*?"

Kasim smirked. Their eyes keep meeting, looking for something hidden deep within.

"You're not hard to miss when you're making the tabloids with Imran, winning awards, attending parties."

Ruhi was about to respond when suddenly—A group of kids ran up to Kasim, tugging at his hand.

"Bhaiya! Ice cream!" they giggled.

Kasim chuckled and walked with them toward the vendor. Ruhi watched him, a strange warmth blooming in her chest.

She hadn't seen him this lighthearted in years. As he handed out the ice cream, the vendor turned to Ruhi and said something that stunned her.

"For the last seven years, Kasim has been coming here, buying ice cream for the kids.

But today is the first time he's had one for himself."

Ruhi's heart skipped a beat. She looked at Kasim, laughing with the children, and suddenly saw him differently. He was someone she admired more than any man she met. His aura was pleasing as this new version of him was attractive in more ways than she could count.

"Let's go," Kasim said, finishing his ice cream.

"Where?"

"It's a surprise."

Ruhi's curiosity piqued as they followed the children down a quiet street, stopping in front of a large old farmhouse.

Ruhi looked around.

"What is this place?"

Kasim just smiled and led her inside. As soon as they entered, a woman greeted them warmly.

"Kasim, I've been waiting for you to come by!"

"Sorry, I've been busy at work," he replied apologetically.

Ruhi stepped farther in, her eyes adjusting to the soft, warm lighting. Children's drawings lined the hallway walls—crayon-colored rainbows, stick figures with wide smiles, and carefully scrawled names in block letters.

Laughter echoed faintly from a nearby room. Her footsteps slowed. Then she saw it—a row of small shoes by the entrance, jackets hung by the door and the distant sound of a lullaby playing. Her chest tightened with sudden clarity.

This wasn't a farmhouse.

It was an *orphanage*.

The caretaker gave Kasim a full update on the children's health, education, and finances while Ruhi observed in quiet awe. She watched the children rush to Kasim, eager to show him their rooms and new toys.

Then, the caretaker turned to Ruhi and smiled.

"Chaudhry Saab has been a godsend. For seven years, he's provided free healthcare for these children.

He and his brother renovated this orphanage, ensuring we didn't shut down. Mahirah ji helps us find good home for the kids.

Kasim Saab, even financially supports the elderly in the old folk's home next door."

Ruhi felt her chest tighten. She had never known this side of him. Then—The caretaker's next words left her speechless.

"You're lucky to have a husband like him."

Ruhi's heart nearly stopped. She turned to correct her—but before she could, the caretaker walked away. Ruhi stood there, frozen.

For the first time… she felt something new. A strange, exhilarating warmth in her chest. Something she had never felt for Kasim before.

Ruhi stood quietly, taking in the colorful walls adorned with cartoon characters. A rare sense of peace settled over her heart. Just then, a young girl in a princess dress approached and shyly asked Ruhi to do her hair.

As Ruhi gently combed through the girl's hair, the child chatted cheerfully about how much she loved living here— how Uncle Kasim, Uncle Daniyal, and Aunt Mahirah threw them birthday parties and made them feel special.

"Will you come to my birthday party next month?" the little girl asked with hopeful eyes.

Ruhi smiled and nodded. "Of course I will."

The girl beamed, kissed Ruhi on the cheek, and skipped away happily, leaving Ruhi with a heart unexpectedly full.

Kasim returned shortly after, wrapping up his visit.

"I'll be back next week with vaccinations for the kids," he said to the caretaker.

They said their goodbyes, then walked back toward the car in comfortable silence. For the first time in years, Ruhi felt truly happy, truly at peace. She wondered—*why hadn't she experienced this kind of happiness before?*

Her career was flourishing, but her busy life never allowed her to give back like this. Had she been so caught up in chasing success that she missed what truly mattered?

They quietly walked, glancing at each other with occasional smiles. No words could describe their feeling as Kasim shared one of the biggest parts of his life. He had never shared this part of his happiness with anyone—never brought anyone to the orphanage. But he knew Ruhi would appreciate it. Years ago, she had encouraged him to give back to those who had little.

Yet somewhere along the way, she had lost that sense of direction.

While Ruhi couldn't express her happiness, she genuinely smiled back with an open heart, believing this was an accomplishment one could only dream of.

A true blessing.

As they reached the car, Ruhi turned to him.

"Who are you?" she asked, half-teasing, half-serious.

Kasim smirked.

"I'm Kasim Chaudhry. Pleasure meeting you." He extended his hand.

Ruhi rolled her eyes but shook it as she lovingly smiled.

"I mean it," she said as she got in the car. "This version of you? I never expected it. I never knew you did any of this."

Kasim shrugged.

"You were right.

God blessed me with more than I needed.

All I knew was…I just want to help others however I can.

Years ago, while I was in med school. I had a patient who couldn't afford to pay his medical bill or afford any medicine.

Eventually, he stopped coming to the clinic, and I was called for a house visit where he cared for these orphanages who couldn't afford anything.

At first, I helped them in small ways; the rest… is history.

133

Ruhi, their blessing *is* the reason I achieved my success."

Ruhi smiled upon hearing his story; Kasim's kindness truly touched her heart.

As they drove home, Ruhi found herself admiring him in a way she never had before. Finally, she found the courage to say—

"Imran and I were never a couple. Not back then, not now!"

Kasim said nothing, but his hands tightened on the steering wheel.

"The media saw us having lunch years ago and assumed we were dating. We never corrected them because the publicity worked for us.

We made occasional lunch meetings and helped each other with contacts.

It was never real.

Or *anything* beyond that!"

Kasim finally glanced at her.

"I know," he said simply.

Ruhi's eyes widened.

"How?"

Kasim just smirked, refusing to answer.

When they reached home, Kasim helped Ruhi out of the car. Before she could say anything, his mother's voice called him inside. He left quickly, but as he did, Ruhi felt an unexpected pain in her heart, as if her heart had broken a little.

She didn't understand why.

And yet, her heart ached for something unknown— something she wished she understood.

She watched him disappear inside, Rehan stood in the distance, watching her from the terrace. He saw the twinkle in her eye.

And Ruhi, without realizing it, smiled back at him as she disappeared inside.

Leaving Rehan worried, whether history could repeat itself.

Dastaan -e- Ishq

Another evening of physiotherapy, and Ruhi pushed herself harder than usual. With deadlines looming and a mountain of unfinished work, she relied on Saira to manage the studio while working with designers to finalize everything. Yet, through it all, Kasim had been her anchor—her steady, unwavering support.

She hadn't truly realized how much he had done for her over the years, never once complaining. Now, more than ever, she longed to fully recover, not just for herself, but to see her commitments through to the very end.

"How much longer until I fully recover?" she asked, hopeful.

Kasim, adjusting her posture, sighed.

"You won't be fully recovered in time for the fashion show," he admitted. "If we rush it, the chances of reinjury are too high."

Ruhi nodded, disappointed but understanding.

"I'll wait then," she said. "I trust you."

With that said, Kasim extends his hand as Ruhi placed her palm into his. The warm sensation of his hand sends shivers down her spine. She felt the world stopped. Time stopped. She gazes in his eyes as he comes behind her as he places his other hand on her hip to provide balance, while holding on to her palm with his other hand to help her walk.

The scent of his pheromones intensifies her longing. She doesn't want him to let go as she places her cheek next to his closing her eyes for a brief second as he directs her toward the bookcase. She opens her eyes with a slight smile looking away as he Kasim releases his hands. Both unable to make eye contact ignoring their repressed feelings.

They continued the session in silence, her breathing slow and measured as she shifted her weight cautiously. The soft creak of the wooden shelf echoed in the quiet room as she reached out to steady herself. Her fingertips skimmed the spines of old books—dusty, worn, familiar.

Suddenly, her hand slipped. She gasped. Kasim moved instinctively, catching her before she could fall. In the scramble, a book tumbled to the floor with a loud thud. As it hit the ground, a folded piece of paper fluttered out like a forgotten whisper.

A letter.

Ruhi settled onto the couch, wincing slightly from the sudden movement. Kasim bent down, picking up the book and the letter. The moment his eyes fell on the handwriting, his breath hitched. He knew this writing. *Anywhere.* Ruhi noticed his change in demeanor.

"Kasim?" she asked, confused.

He turned to her, holding up the letter.

"This... this is my aunt's Asma's handwriting."

Ruhi's eyes widened.

His deceased aunt. The woman whose death had torn their families apart. Kasim sat beside Ruhi, his hands slightly shaking as he unfolded the letter.

Together, they read the words that had been lost for decades.

Noman,

I'm sorry my family and I pushed you to marry me when you didn't want to.

It was unfair to you.

I knew all along that you were in love with someone else. I felt helpless and couldn't speak up. But I know now that I should have stood up to my brother.

And you had no choice but to reject me.

You did right and stood by the woman, your love.

I'm sorry it caused a rift in our families.

But I want you to know—I am happy for you.

I know you are a good man, and I know you'll blame yourself.

Please don't.

And don't worry about me. My brother found me a wonderful man. I will say yes to the proposal. I think it's best for both of us to move forward.

With time, I will convince my family, and things will go back to normal. I promise....

I wish you all the best.

Asma

Kasim and Ruhi exchanged stunned looks.

"She didn't…" Ruhi's voice trailed off, realization dawning.

"Commit suicide," Kasim finished, his voice hollow with shock.

His aunt had moved on. She had forgiven. She had never held hatred in her heart. Yet, their families had spent years drowning in anger and grief over a false belief. Without wasting another second, they knew what they had to do.

Kasim and Ruhi rushed home, the letter clutched tightly in his hand. The moment they entered, they found Rehan in his study.

Kasim wordlessly handed him the letter.

Rehan's hands, which had once been so firm and unshakable, trembled as he held the fragile paper. He read the words slowly. His face paled. His lips parted, but no words came out.

The man who had held onto his pain for decades now sat in stunned silence. His wife, standing nearby, spoke first.

"It's time to let this go, Rehan," she said gently.

"We lost her," she continued. "But we can't keep losing more because of a misunderstanding."

Kasim stood beside his father.

"Abba, it's time to end this feud."

Something inside Rehan broke. Without saying a word, he stood up. And walked straight toward Omar's house.

Everyone followed nervously.

What was he going to do?

Would this finally end in peace… or more destruction?

Without knocking, Rehan walked into Omar's home.

Sitting at the dining table, Omar and his wife stood up. Their eyes locked.

The atmosphere shifted.

A moment of heavy silence. Then—

Rehan placed the letter in Omar's hands.

Omar read it, his hands gripping the edges of the paper tightly. His wife read over his shoulder, a small gasp escaping her lips.

When he finished, Omar looked up. His eyes glossed with unshed tears. And in that moment, nothing needed to be said.

They had both lost.

They had both suffered.

And they had both been wrong.

Tears fell silently as the two former best friends embraced. The pain of decades melted away in that moment. Forgiveness replaced it.

Closure finally arrived.

And for the first time in twenty years—

There was peace.

DASTAAN -E- ISHQ

With their families reunited, Kasim and Ruhi's friendship had found its old rhythm. Laughter echoed in both houses. Dinners were shared, stories exchanged, and old wounds finally healed.

Omar and Rehan had discovered a renewed friendship. They knew their pride had cost them years of peace, yet their mutual understanding had never truly faded. The shame of their past actions lingered like a shadow, but in time, they made peace with it—and finally laid the past to rest.

As Ruhi prepared for her fashion show, the mothers reminded her that right after the event, they would be throwing Mahirah's baby shower.

Ruhi smiled, promising she wouldn't miss it.

One afternoon, as Omar and Rehan played chess, Omar spoke thoughtfully.

"I'm proud of both Kasim and Daniyal," he admitted.

"They've carved their own paths, built their own names, and gained respect in their fields."

He smiled.

"And the work they do—caring for orphans and the elderly—is incredible. Their achievements speak for themselves."

Rehan nodded, placing a hand on one of the chess pieces but not making a move.

"It wouldn't have been possible without you."

Omar raised a brow.

"What do you mean?"

Rehan smirked.

"I know you were the one who encouraged Kasim to pursue medicine."

Omar froze.

Rehan leaned back in his chair, the smirk never leaving his face.

"I know because I overheard your conversation with Kasim seven years ago."

Omar's eyes widened.

146

Rehan continued, "That day, when Kasim bought his pre-med books, he thought he had cut the call.

But he accidentally accepted it instead.

I heard everything."

Omar sat back, speechless. Then, after a moment, he chuckled.

"Well, then, I suppose you also know that you and Reshma ran to the hospital the second you heard Ruhi had fallen."

Rehan let out a small laugh.

"Touche...And Checkmate!"

Before they could say anything else, Ruhi walked in.

"You two need to wrap this up because you're all coming to my fashion show," she announced.

They exchanged a glance before nodding.

"Of course, we will," Rehan said.

Just then, Ruhi's phone rang. Her expression changed.

Something was wrong at the studio. She grabbed her things, preparing to leave, but Omar stopped her.

"Take Kasim with you. You're still injured."

Before Ruhi could protest, Kasim was already beside her. The moment they arrived at the studio, Imran was waiting. His eyes darkened at the sight of Kasim beside Ruhi.

With fake politeness, Imran greeted Kasim.

"Ah, so you're Ruhi's personal chaperone now?" he said mockingly.

Kasim was about to respond, but Ruhi reached out and gently grabbed his hand, stopping him. He looked at her and smiled—a simple gesture, yet enough to make Imran's jaw tighten with restrained frustration.

Ruhi, however, met Imran's gaze with a stern look. She had grown tired of his condescending nature. She knew that causing a scene now—especially with investors arriving for a brief meeting—could damage her reputation, branding her as unprofessional.

But in that moment, Imran's arrogance no longer mattered.

What mattered was Kasim—how he would respond. Would he retaliate with anger?

Ruhi let go of her internal struggle and turned to Kasim with a calm smile, silently assuring him: *I'm in good hands.*

Silently, he leaves.

Ruhi met with her investors, who commended her dedication despite her injury. She introduced Kasim, and the investors thanked him for helping Ruhi recover.

It was only then that Imran finally realized—

Kasim wasn't just a friend.

He was Ruhi's physician.

For the first time, Imran looked uncertain. He thought he needed to handle the situation once more as his future felt slipping away.

Ruhi was an asset that he couldn't lose.

He needed a plan.

As the day went on, Ruhi grew overwhelmed with

preparations. Imran saw this as an opportunity. He swooped in, offering fake concern.

"I'm here for you, Ruhi," he said smoothly.

Before he could say more, Kasim stepped away, answering a phone call.

Ruhi, unmoved by Imran's words, shook her head.

"Thank you for your concern, but Saira and I have everything under control."

Imran's smile faltered. He knew there wasn't much he could do at this time, but he'd think of something. By the time Kasim returned, Imran had left but kept a close watch from nearby.

Kasim turned to Ruhi.

"I took a few days off from work," he told her.

"I'll help you with the fashion show. Like old times."

Ruhi smiled but shook her head.

"You don't have to do that, Kasim. You've already done

more than enough."

Kasim's expression remained firm.

"No. I want to be here."

Before Ruhi could say anything, a coworker called her. She excused herself, leaving Kasim alone. The second she was out of sight, Imran reappeared. He walked up to Kasim, voice low and smug.

"I know this 'nice guy' act," Imran sneered.

"It didn't work then, and it's not going to work now." He continued.

Kasim turned to face him, his expression unreadable. Kasim responded to the sneer with a smile.

"I have no idea what you're talking about," he said calmly.

"But if you know what's good for you, you'll back off."

Imran laughed.

"You were a fool then, and you're a fool now.

I've worked too hard for you to come back and distract Ruhi."

Kasim's calm exterior cracked.

"All you've ever done is *use* her."

His voice was low, controlled—but filled with quiet fury.

"You've built your entire career on *her* success.

Without Ruhi, you'd be *nothing*.

If you hadn't modeled in those college fashion shows, you wouldn't have gotten anywhere....

She handed you this career on a silver platter." Kasim continued.

Imran's smirk dropped.

"Don't you ever forget that!" Kasim said leaning close, speaking in his ear.

Before he could respond, Ruhi returned, sensing the tension.

"What's going on?" she asked, her eyes narrowing.

Imran was the first to respond, but his voice was too smooth.

"Nothing.

We were just remembering our college days," he added.

Kasim said nothing, but as he passed Imran, he shoulder-bummed him.

Ruhi watched Kasim walk away. Something felt off. She glanced at Imran, who avoided her gaze.

Imran feared Kasim's return. He knew the growing closeness between Kasim and Ruhi could cost him everything—even his career. He had to tread carefully. And so, with the same cunning that once served him before, his mind began crafting a new plan—one that would once again shift Ruhi's attention away from Kasim.

Doubt crept into Ruhi's mind as she felt the two men wanted to tear each other apart if she hadn't shown up. She thought these two could at least be civil.

At that moment, her internal feelings nudged her to stay true to herself. She assured herself that she had trusted the right person all along.

DASTAAN -E- ISHQ

For the next few days, Ruhi worked tirelessly, pouring her heart and soul into the fashion show. And just like old times, Kasim was right beside her, helping her every step of the way. But there was one person who was far from thrilled. Imran.

His insecurities burned, watching Ruhi and Kasim together laughing, working, and sharing stolen glances. The more Ruhi's eyes searched for Kasim, the more Imran fumed. She was in pain, yet she refused to rest despite Kasim's constant nagging for her to take it easy. But she wouldn't stop. This show meant everything to her. And so did Kasim.

Finally, the night of the fashion show arrived. The venue was breathtaking, the energy electric. When Kasim arrived, he was dressed in a pure white shalwar kameez. Ruhi looked nothing short of stunning in a simple yet elegant white lehenga. Their matching outfits didn't go unnoticed.

Everyone complimented how perfect they looked together— Except for Imran. He watched silently as they received attention to Kasim than him. A coworker excitedly suggested a picture of them together. Ruhi, feeling shy, kept refusing.

Until—

Kasim placed his hand on her waist, pulling her to his side. She stiffened for a second, startled by the sudden heat of his touch—

Then, their eyes met, and the moment froze.

Something shifted as they were lost in each other's simile. The flash of the camera snapped them back to reality. Ruhi blushed furiously and quickly walked away. Kasim, watching her flustered retreat, smirked to himself.

As the fashion show started, Ruhi's team, Kasim, and her family were thrilled. It was finally happening. Their hard work was about to pay off. It was evident excitement and happiness filled the room. All showed their gratitude except for one person.

Imran.

He was restless, looking for any excuse to distract Ruhi. But Kasim saw right through him.

Every time Imran tried, Kasim was there—saving Ruhi from every little disruption, mistake, or excuse. Though completely focused on her show, Ruhi couldn't help but constantly search for Kasim as they worked. And every time she found him, their eyes met.

They exchanged small, knowing smiles like they were the only two people in the room. It was unspoken. And it was driving Imran insane.

The show was a success. It was truly a one-of-a-kind fashion show, making history by reuniting famous television couples on stage. Every model, every design, every detail was executed flawlessly. Everything was perfect.

Until—

Imran stumbled on stage during his ramp walk. Embarrassed and furious, he smiled through his horror, thinking his career was over. To his surprise, the crowd still showed him love, but his relentless nature sought revenge.

The final showstopper celebrity couple was presented on the stage as Imran took advantage of the situation. He stared at Ruhi's cane, knowing she'd have to give a speech.

"No cane, No speech." He said as he snatched the cane, breaking it on his knee and tossing it on the side before her speech.

As the show ended, the sponsors and hosts invited Ruhi to the stage to give a speech. Her staff looked for the cane but could not find it until someone noticed it was broken. They thought it had been broken accidentally by someone.

Ruhi thought her moment had passed as she couldn't walk properly. Without her cane, she was stuck. Panicked, she turned to Saira.

"You'll have to give the speech instead," Ruhi whispered as the announcer called her name.

Imran watched from the stage, smirking. Before Saira could respond—

Kasim stepped in.

"No."

Before anyone could react, he scooped Ruhi into his arms. The entire venue gasped. Imran was furious watching them. Kasim walked through the stage, carrying her effortlessly toward the center of the stage.

He was calm, confident, and completely unbothered by the thousands of eyes watching. But his eyes were on Ruhi as he walked. Ruhi's breath hitched. She stared back at him, unable to look away.

His intense gaze made her forget everything—The show, the audience, the cameras. There was only Kasim. With each step, their heart twined into one. No care in the world; it was only this moment.

Imran, standing in the shadows, clenched his fists. He could feel it—his status slipping, his relevance fading. He knew he failed, and it was all because of Kasim.

The crowd erupted into applause.

Kasim smiled down at Ruhi as he gently placed her on the stage. He handed her the mic, his eyes gleaming with pride. And as the crowd continued to cheer, Ruhi turned to him—

Watching him clap was the hardest for her. She smiled with her whole heart, watching him. As the applause faded, Ruhi took a deep breath.

And then—she spoke.

"I want to thank everyone for giving me the opportunity to create this iconic fashion show."

The crowd cheered.

"I want to thank all the celebrity participants, my coworkers, my co-partner Saira… my family, and everyone who made this night possible."

Then—

She turned to Kasim. And before she could stop herself, she grabbed his hand.

The crowd gasped.

"But most of all, I want to thank you."

She looked directly into Kasim's eyes.

"Dr. Kasim Ali Chaudhry."

Kasim's breath caught. Ruhi's voice softened.

"You went above and beyond to help me get to where I am

today."

A small pause.

"As I stand here tonight, it is because of your dedication and support that I was able to make this show a success despite my injury."

A deep emotion flickered in Kasim's eyes.

Ruhi smiled.

"As I stand here in front of all of you, it is his dedication to his work that helped me continue my work for this fashion show with this foot injury. So… thank you for being my doctor, my best friend…my hero, Kasim Chaudhry.

And for making this night possible."

The crowd exploded into applause. Mahirah and Daniyal cheered the hardest from the coward with their families watching. Ruhi was lost in Kasim's eyes as she saw him applauding; at this moment, his happiness was hers, and they couldn't take their eyes off each other.

Imran watched from the sidelines, his worst fear unfolding

before his eyes. He had lost. Not just the spotlight. But Ruhi. The one thing he had worked so hard to keep in his grasp. And as the audience continued to cheer for Kasim and Ruhi—

One thing became clear.

This was only the beginning.

***

After the success of the fashion show, Ruhi, beaming with joy, invited Saira and Kasim to a celebratory dinner at a restaurant. Ruhi's joy was evident. It was the first time in a long time that she wanted to celebrate her success with someone. As they sat at the table, Ruhi slid an envelope across to them.

"Here," she said, smiling.

Saira furrowed her brows. "What's this?"

"A gift," Ruhi replied. "For both of you."

Kasim hesitated. "There's no need for this. I didn't do this for money."

Ruhi scoffed, shaking her head.

"Saira, you've earned this. You put in so much time and effort into the show."

She then turned to Kasim.

"And for you, the money isn't for you personally—it's for your charities. My contribution to the orphanage and the old folk's home."

Kasim opened his mouth to protest, but Ruhi raised a hand.

"I'm not taking no for an answer."

She forced the envelope into his hand.

Reluctantly, both Kasim and Saira accepted. The night ended on a high note, and Kasim offered to drop them home. But first, he excused himself to use the restroom.

The girls made their way toward the parking lot, laughter and excitement still lingering in the air—

Imran appeared alone, drunk, and furious. The atmosphere changed instantly. His eyes were bloodshot, and his steps were unstable. His rage burned through his intoxicated haze.

Ruhi and Saira stood frozen in fear, clutching each other's hands as a drunken Imran staggered toward them. His rage was unmistakable—they could see it in his eyes. And they knew he meant business.

"You planned my humiliation, didn't you?!" he shouted, his voice slurring as he grabbed Ruhi's arm.

Ruhi jerked back.

"What is your problem?!" she demanded.

Saira shoved Imran away. "Let go of her!"

Imran stumbled but didn't back down.

"You think I need you?" he scoffed, grabbing her arm again, his words unsteady as she fought him.

"I don't. I'm a superstar."

SLAP.

Ruhi's hand connected with his face in a sharp, resounding hit.

The parking lot fell silent. Imran's head snapped to the side. His cheeks burned with humiliation.

"You think you can do this just because Kasim is back in your life?!"

He lunged for her. But before he could touch her—A fist collided with his face from the side.

Imran staggered back, clutching his jaw.

Kasim.

Standing in front of Ruhi, fury flashing in his eyes.

"How dare you lay a hand on her?" Kasim's voice was deadly calm.

PUNCH

"If you ever touch her again, I will break every bone in your body."

Ruhi placed a hand on Kasim's arm.

"It's okay," she said softly. "He's drunk."

Kasim's jaw clenched as he turns but couldn't help himself.

SLAP.

Another hit—this time, from Kasim. Imran stumbled back, eyes burning with hatred.

Then—

He smirked.

"I should have done worse than injuring her foot," Imran said, laughing as he lay on the pavement.

Ruhi's eyes widened. Kasim froze.

"What?" Ruhi whispered, her voice shaking.

Imran laughed bitterly.

"I threw oil on the floor that day," he admitted, his voice laced with malice. He slowly got up, stumbling, laughing hysterically.

"That's what caused your accident.

Payback.

For ruining my career. For taking away my chance at becoming an international movie star.

You stole *my* opportunity.

So, I wanted to ruin you." Imran laughter echoed through the parking lot.

The rage in Kasim's eyes was uncontrollable.

PUNCH.

This time, harder. Imran stumbled back again, his lip split and bleeding.

A click.

Saira had been recording everything.

Imran's confession.

His crime.

His desperation.

She held up her phone, smirking. Imran's eyes widened as he spit blood on the floor laughing hysterically.

"The world is about to see your true face, Imran." Imran continued to laugh hysterically as Kasim held his neck, slamming him on the hood of the car.

Ruhi never seen this side of Kasim as he continues to punch Imran senselessly.

Moments later, the police arrived, storming toward them. Unable to pull Kasim away as he held tightly onto Imran's neck. Finally, Kasim came back to reality as three guards held him back.

"I broke your foot…. I destroyed your…" Imran continued to laugh hysterically as Kasim held his neck, pushing him on the hood of the car and punching him.

Moments later, the police arrived, storming toward them.

"Mr. Imran Ali, you're under arrest."

Handcuffs clicked around his wrists. The sound of his laughter continued to echo as he struggled, but the officers forced him inside the police car.

As the car drove away, Kasim turned to Ruhi. She was stunned, still processing everything. Kasim placed a hand on her shoulder.

"It's over. Let's go home!"

Ruhi exhaled, looking into his steady, unwavering eyes. For the first time in her life, a man made her feel completely safe.

Dastaan -e- Ishq

ACT FOUR

A month passed, and Ruhi and Kasim spent more time together than ever. To their surprise, they've gotten closer than before. Ruhi had fully recovered from her injury and found true joy in helping Kasim with the orphanage and the old folk's home. Her love for helping the children and the elderly ignited a new strength within her. With Kasim by her side, she knew she could accomplish anything.

On the other hand, Reshma was busy preparing for Mahirah's baby shower and assigned Kasim, Ruhi, and Saira to take charge of decorations. Together, they worked tirelessly, planning a lavish celebration for Mahirah and Daniyal. During the preparations, Saira decided to choreograph a dance sequence for the event, and to everyone's delight, she paired Kasim and Ruhi.

The baby shower was spectacular, with laughter, love, and celebration filling the room. When the dance performance began, all eyes were on Kasim and Ruhi as they danced in perfect harmony.

The chemistry between them was undeniable, and the guests couldn't stop cheering and applauding. After the performance, Ruhi noticed Saira and Kasim deep in conversation. A strange feeling twisted in her chest, tightening like a knot. Her throat grew dry, and a slow burn spread beneath her ribs. For the first time, she felt jealous.

The night's festivities continued as Kasim and Ruhi enjoyed each other's company over dinner while the rest of the guests mingled. From a distance, Daniyal and Mahirah spotted them and decided to join.

"I can't thank you enough for this baby shower," Mahirah said, hugging Ruhi from behind as Daniyal sat beside Kasim.

"You both were outstanding. How did you organize all this while still caring for everything at the orphanage?" Daniyal asked.

"Well, I had an assistant," Kasim said with a smile, glancing at Ruhi as she helped Mahirah sit.

"I'm incredibly proud of what you both have accomplished at the orphanage. It's truly remarkable," Ruhi said, addressing the boys.

"Kasim's volunteering and getting us involved in small projects is why God heard our prayers and blessed us with a child," Mahirah said warmly.

She turned to Ruhi. "You know, not being able to conceive was my greatest heartbreak. But somehow, we were led to these children—to make their lives better.

Over the past three years, the joy I've felt spending time with them, reading to them, and cooking for them... brought us closer.

As a child psychologist, I feel I must help them in the best way possible." She reached for Daniyal's hand.

Daniyal noticed Ruhi eyeing Kasim, who stared back at her.

"So, Ruhi…" Daniyal smirked. "Tell me, is there someone in your life? You're an attractive woman—I'm sure you get approached often."

Ruhi smiled, her gaze flickering toward Kasim. "No, there's no one."

Kasim, feigning indifference, looked off into the distance.

"Kasim," Mahirah said playfully, "Ma and I have been looking for the perfect girl for you. We'd love to introduce you to someone."

"Nah, Bhabhi," Kasim said with a chuckle.

"I love my work too much—spending time with my patients, taking care of them, and then there's the orphanage and the elderly home—" He glanced at Ruhi mid-sentence.

"All of that will still be there," Mahirah teased. "But tell me, what are you looking for? It might help us narrow the search a little."

Daniyal grinned mischievously.

"I already know what he's looking for."

Kasim raised a brow. "Oh? And what's that?"

Daniyal pointed at the tree, referencing an old tale about a witch who supposedly lived there. A burst of laughter followed.

"You were so afraid of that tree," Ruhi said, grinning.

"That's because he kept telling me the witch would come to take me if I didn't behave," Kasim replied.

"And you actually believed him?" Mahirah asked, amused.

"Yeah, I was four!" Kasim defended. "He also told me, the white stones on the marble floor were diamonds. I grabbed a little hammer to break the floor and dig them out.

Instead, Abba came *running* after me—with his sandals."

They all laughed as Kasim fondly recalled their childhood mischief. Daniyal seized the perfect moment to swipe food from his brother's plate, and the two broke into a playful scuffle over the meal.

"Now, seriously, Kasim. Tell me what you're looking for," Mahirah asked.

"I don't know. I haven't really thought about it," Kasim replied.

"Sure, you have. Every guy has," Daniyal said, stuffing his face with samosas from Kasim's plate.

"Oh really? Was that before or after you married me?" Mahirah asked, raising an eyebrow.

"After... I mean, before... Ah, you know what I mean," Daniyal stammered as Mahirah glared at him.

"Okay, my dear wife, if you must know the truth—when we met in college a hundred years ago, I already had an image of you in my mind long before that," Daniyal said with a grin.

"Really? An image of how she looked, or her personality?" Ruhi asked, intrigued.

"Both, actually.

Of course, I wanted to marry someone beautiful, but more

than that, I *wanted* someone kind and thoughtful. Someone who took care of everyone around her." Daniyal glanced at Mahirah fondly.

"You know, she had this friend, Nabeel, and I thought something was going on—"

"And he hated him," Mahirah cut in with a laugh. "Poor guy got bullied by Daniyal constantly."

"Because I was jealous!" Daniyal admitted.

"He hogged all your time and attention. I was madly in love with you from the moment I saw you in the cafeteria, feeding the janitor's son.

I thought about *how thoughtful and kind she was.*

And then came Nabeel—smart, intelligent, kind, just like her.

And I was *terrified* she'd never even notice me."

"So... tell me, how did you two become college sweethearts?" Ruhi asked, amused.

"Well," Mahirah began, "one day, I had to stay late at college for a project. Meanwhile, Daniyal was getting scolded by Professor Jangir for bullying Nabeel in class."

Ruhi's eyes widened. "What did he do?"

"He threw ink on Nabeel—as a joke," Mahirah said, shaking her head.

"The fountain pen broke," Daniyal defended himself with a wicked smile.

"That day, Nabeel left his books behind because of an emergency and rushed home. Everyone assumed it was because of Daniyal, but it was something else entirely," Mahirah continued.

"I decided to take his books to his house since he lived right behind the school. What I didn't know was that Daniyal had followed me…"

"I wanted to make sure you were safe," Daniyal interjected.

"Sure…" Mahirah replied, raising a skeptical brow.

"So, when I followed her—not because I was jealous, but

because I *feared for her safety*—I discovered the truth," Daniyal explained.

"Nabeel's father had suffered a heart attack, and his younger brother was home alone. His father... was our college janitor.

"Oh, I felt awful about how I had treated him. I learned that Nabeel had been struggling all along.

His father worked at our college to reduce his tuition fees and could only afford to send his younger son to a local school.

Meanwhile, Nabeel worked part-time after attending university to ease his father's burden.

That was a life-changing moment for me."

"What you did afterward won my heart..." Mahirah said softly.

Kasim, now intrigued, leaned forward.

"What did you do?"

Daniyal sighed.

"I ran to Abba and told him everything. That day, I received the *best* slap of my life."

Kasim chuckled.

"Abba's slaps are powerful—I should know."

Daniyal smirked before continuing, "Abba was ruthless, and Ma did not support me either.

'I thought I raised you better than this,' Abba said.

'All this time, you mocked him without ever considering what he might be going through.

So, what if he couldn't afford luxuries like you?

So, what if he rode a bicycle instead of a car?

He works *hard* for everything he has. Even if it's not enough for you!

And I did, too, when I was your age.

When Omar and I came here, all we had was 500 rupees. We

built our lives from nothing. I always taught you to respect hard work.'

"I felt ashamed," Daniyal admitted.

"But that's not what won me over," Mahirah teased.

"Oh, come on. The rest is history," Daniyal said, suddenly shy.

"I want to know," Ruhi insisted.

"Do tell... Now I *really* want to know," Kasim added, smirking as Daniyal turned red.

"He took all his savings, anonymously paid Nabeel's father's medical bills, and even covered his brother's tuition—getting him admitted into one of the best schools in the city. He did all of this without letting Nabeel or his father know," Mahirah said, squeezing Daniyal's hand as she gazed at him.

"But wait... how did you find out?" Ruhi asked, curious.

"I went to pick up Nabeel's younger brother from school one day because Nabeel had to work. That's when I saw Daniyal paying his tuition," Mahirah said.

"So, I did what I do best—I confronted him."

"And like a nervous criminal, I spilled everything," Daniyal admitted.

"You should've seen his face—he was so nervous," Mahirah laughed.

"Why do I feel like there's more to this?" Kasim asked, narrowing his eyes.

"There's nothing more... and they lived happily ever after. *The end,*" Daniyal said quickly.

"Well... not quite yet," Mahirah teased.

"Oh, come on..." Daniyal groaned.

"I *want* to know! Do tell," Ruhi urged.

Mahirah smiled. "I began to see him in a different light. He was kinder—not just to Nabeel, but to others.

He started asking about my day.

...ven read me poetry," she said as Daniyal covered his face with his hands.

"Poetry," Kasim said with a laugh, grabbing Daniyal's shoulders as his brother buried his face in embarrassment.

"But what I appreciated most was that he made an effort to walk me to the bus stop every day, always asking me the same question: *'Let me drop you home.'*

And every time, I'd say, *'I live in a small community... people will make up stories about us.'*

But he would just smile and say, *'Let them.'"*

Ruhi sighed dreamily.

"Over time, we started spending more time together. But I became afraid..."

"Why?" Kasim asked.

"Because he was rich, and I was poor," Mahirah admitted.

"So what? That doesn't matter," Ruhi said firmly.

"But it did to me at the time. I was trapped in the

expectations of society and culture… I forgot that there ʋ good people in the world.

I was told from a young age that people marry within their social status. So, I focused on my education.

I was the only child of a widowed father who worked as a train conductor. Abba worked tirelessly to put me through private school, and I earned a scholarship to university.

All I ever wanted was to make him proud.

One day, I built up the courage to ask Daniyal a question. And the rest… was history," Mahirah said, smiling at Daniyal as they held hands.

"So, you proposed?" Ruhi asked.

"Yes and no," Mahirah replied. "He asked me, *'When should I come to your house with my parents?'*

In return, I asked him a question—a test. I knew his response would either make us or break us.

And to my surprise, his answer wasn't what I expected."

"I'm sure my brother aced the test," Kasim said. "If he didn't, you wouldn't be sitting here."

Daniyal grinned, placing his arm around Mahirah.

"Why don't you ask Kasim? Let's see how *Mr. Overconfident* responds."

"I'm sure his answer will be the same," Mahirah said confidently.

"You think so?" Daniyal challenged.

Mahirah turned to Kasim.

"Okay, tell me…. What would you do if the love of your life was an only child, and she wanted to work—not for herself, but to give her income to her father after marriage?

Or even *your* income because she wanted to take care of him?"

Kasim thought for a moment before answering.

"Well, I think if she wants to work, it should be for herself, not for others. Don't get me wrong—women should work for their self-respect and independence.

If a man can build a career with the support of his wife, then why can't a woman do the same? She should have something of her own that defines her.

Women are more than just wives, daughters, or mothers. We shouldn't box them *in* as a society—we should let them live and breathe.

As for money... I would never be the kind of husband who expects his wife to hand over her paycheck. She earned it; she can keep it.

In fact, I believe every woman should have her own separate bank account.

If my wife wants me to come home and hand my entire salary to her, I *will*.

If she wants me to put the house in her name, I *will*.

Because a house only becomes a *home* when the wife or mother of the house is happy."

Kasim paused for a moment before continuing as Daniyal

and Mahirah smiled at each other.

"And about *in-laws*—I think it's one of the most ridiculous terms in the world. If a wife can call her mother-in-law *'mother'* in our culture, then why can't a husband call his father-in-law' *father'?*

"If my wife wants to give her salary to her father, I wouldn't stop her.

How could I?

In fact, I would contribute as much as I could—not because he's my father-in-law, but because he's *my father, too.*

And if, in the future, my wife's parents ever needed us, I wouldn't even think twice—I'd move them in with us. No discussion needed."

Kasim finished speaking, his eyes lingering on Ruhi like a quiet storm released just behind his gaze.

She gazed back at him, her heart swelling with admiration. She had always known Kasim was a kind man, but today, her respect for him soared beyond words.

"I *told* you he's one of us," Daniyal said, grinning as he high-fived his brother.

"You two surprise me," Mahirah said, shaking her head. "You think so much alike, yet you're so different at the same time. Daniyal gave the *exact* same response."

Just then, Saira approached the table.

"Kasim, some guests are asking for you," she said.

Kasim nodded and left with her, laughing and chatting as they walked away.

Ruhi watched them, but suddenly, a strange feeling crept into her heart.

Something felt wrong.

As the night continued Mahirah, observed Ruhi's expression, she smirked knowingly. Deciding to distract her, Mahirah pulled Ruhi into the kitchen to help prepare snacks for everyone. As they worked, Mahirah casually brought up Kasim.

"You *need* to confess your feelings to him," she said,

observing Ruhi.

Ruhi froze.

"There's nothing between us," she said too quickly.

Mahirah raised a brow. *"Really?"*

Ruhi avoided her knowing gaze, focusing on placing snacks on the tray.

"Yeah, he's my friend," Ruhi said as Daniyal enters holding presents.

"I said the same thing years ago. Mahirah and I were friends and always will be.

But the sad truth that I had to accept was that she was the only girl I couldn't just be friends with, I wanted more.

We wanted more," Daniyal said as he stood beside his wife, putting his arm around her.

"Look, no will blame you if—" Daniyal continued as Ruhi softly spoke.

"It's really nothing. Kasim and I are best friends; he

189

understands me and gives me the respect I—"

Mahirah interjected as Daniyal smiled.

"If that's not love, then what is?"

Deep down, Ruhi knew Mahirah was right. But she wasn't ready to admit it. Meanwhile, Rehan and Omar sat together in the living room, reminiscing about old friends and the peace they had finally found.

"It's time for a new beginning," Rehan said, sipping his tea.

Omar nodded in agreement. Without hesitation, Rehan spoke—

"I want to ask for Saira's hand in marriage for Kasim."

The words echoed through the house as Ruhi and Mahirah entered at that moment, snacks in hand. The room fell silent. Rehan words echoed through the room shattering Ruhi into pieces.

"I know what you'll say, but it's all in the past. We love Saira, and she'll be a good match for Kasim."

Ruhi's heart stopped.

Omar briefly considered the proposal before responding, "It's not up to me to say yes, but I'll speak to Saira's family and ask her."

The entire family erupted with joy at the suggestion. Everyone except Ruhi. But she smiled through the pain. Moments later, Kasim and Saira entered together.

Rehan looked at Kasim.

"Do you like Saira?"

Kasim, unaware of Ruhi's presence, smiled.

"Yes," he said without hesitation.

Ruhi's chest tightened as she held her tears with a smile. Everyone turned to Saira. She glanced at Kasim before nodding shyly, breaking Ruhi's heart.

Omar wasted no time.

He called his sister, Saira's mother, and the family quickly agreed to the marriage proposal.

The room was filled with congratulations, hugs, and excitement. Saira turned to Ruhi, who quickly pulled her into a tight hug, holding back her tears as best she could. Her mind raced as her eyes fell on Kasim—smiling, joyful, wrapped in the embrace of his brother and father.

But Ruhi—

She felt like she couldn't breathe.

Ruhi's phone rang, and she used it as an excuse to leave the room. She stepped outside, her hands shaking.

And then—

She ran.

Straight into her house.

Straight into the bathroom.

She turned on the faucet, letting the water drown out her sobs. She cried uncontrollably, her heart shattering into pieces.

Every moment with Kasim—every laugh, every smile, every

look— Flashed before her eyes.

She had fallen in love with him.

And now—it was too late. Ruhi rejection of Kasim seven years ago had come full circle.

Now, she felt rejected.

She has *fallen* as he said she would, and he's not there to catch her.

Wiping her tears, Ruhi fixed herself, put on a blank expression, and went downstairs. Her family had already returned from Kasim's house, buzzing with excitement about the engagement.

Ruhi's mind raced as she headed downstairs, maintaining her simile and happiness. But deep down, she knew she had to escape, and before she could stop herself—

She blurted out, "I've been offered a project in Dubai… I'll be leaving soon."

The room fell silent.

Saira's face immediately fell. Out of anger, she stormed upstairs. Her parents, furious, scolded her.

"You're choosing your career over your family—again!" her mother snapped.

Ruhi swallowed the lump in her throat and nodded.

"I've already accepted the job."

"Is that more *important* to you?" Omar asked.

"Please, Abu—" Ruhi responded, pleading with him to let her run.

"NO!" Yelled Omar as silence roamed the room.

"Who is Saira to you? How could you do this to her?

She's been by your side every step of the way, and you'll desert her when she needs you the most.

Ruhi, this world of glamour has robbed you of your values." Omar said as her parents left, disappointed.

Ruhi, emotionally exhausted, walked to Saira's room. She sat down beside her, not saying anything.

Saira finally spoke.

"If you want to leave, I won't stop you."

Her voice was flat, emotionless.

"But I would have liked my sister and best friend with me for my engagement."

Ruhi's heart ached. She knew it would be cruel to leave Saira, as her parents were right.

Taking a deep breath, she said, "Okay. I'll stay... but only until the engagement."

Saira's mood instantly lifted.

"Good! We'll have to go shopping in a few days!" she said, smiling.

Ruhi forced herself to nod and smile. But deep down—she was breaking.

At that moment, her phone rang.

Kasim.

Her fingers hovered over the screen. But instead of answering—

She ignored the call.

And at that moment, she knew she had to distance herself from Kasim. For their happiness, she'll have to leave.

***

In the days that followed, Ruhi did everything she could to avoid Kasim. She buried herself in work, focusing on her new project and ensuring she was too busy to visit Kasim's house.

Even when he stopped by, she would pretend to be in an important meeting, keeping her door shut. At night, he stood on his balcony, throwing pebbles at her window, just as she used to do to him.

But she never came out.

Even though she was awake, crying, she refused to let him see her pain. Kasim wasn't blind. He sensed something was wrong but couldn't understand why Ruhi was avoiding him.

Had he done something wrong?

Had he hurt her unknowingly?

The more he thought about it, the more frustrated he became. He wished to know what was going on in Ruhi's mind and why there was a sudden change in attitude and distance.

The next day arrived, but the heaviness in Ruhi's heart remained as it was. Unable to concentrate on her work, Saira and Ruhi decided to go shopping for the engagement, and Kasim decided to meet them at the mall. Ruhi knew to avoid Kasim at all costs.

They quickly arrive at the mall feeling as if she didn't belong. Her heartache was unbearable as she was lost in her own world. Kasim arrives; he devotes his attention to Saira instead of Ruhi, leaving her insecure.

Saira and Kasim shopped together, laughing and exchanging opinions on outfits. Ruhi watched from afar, her heart aching, but she kept a fake smile.

Kasim tried including Ruhi; whenever he tried to speak to her, she found an excuse to walk away. She was mastering the art of avoidance. But Kasim wasn't letting it go.

While browsing outfits in a shop, Ruhi's fingers absentmindedly skimmed over the intricate embroidery of a dress. That's when Kasim appeared. Standing right beside her. She froze. There was nowhere to run this time.

"Is everything okay?" he asked, his voice low but firm.

Ruhi forced herself to smile.

"Yeah," she lied.

Kasim's gaze didn't waver.

"Then why are you avoiding me?"

"I'm not," Ruhi said quickly, still pretending to browse.

"Just been busy with a new project and preparing for the engagement."

Kasim's eyes darkened slightly. He studied her carefully, searching for something she wasn't saying. Ruhi kept browsing; he grabbed her hand as she stopped.

Then—he asked a simple question.

"Are you happy?"

Ruhi's breath hitched.

Her mask cracked for a split second, but she quickly forced a smile.

"Yeah, I am."

She turned to him, her smile too bright, too fake.

"My best friends are getting engaged; why wouldn't I be," she said, forcing enthusiasm into her voice.

Kasim didn't believe her.

But he didn't press.

Instead, his gaze lingered on her for a moment as if reading between the lines. Then—without breaking eye contact, he reached to the side, grabbed a lavender and silver outfit, and handed it to her. And just like that—

He walked away.

Leaving Ruhi speechless, holding the outfit in her trembling hands.

***

The night before the engagement was heavy, the air thick with unspoken words and unshed tears. Rehan's family invited Omar and his family for dinner. Mahirah and Daniyal decorated the house for the guests, making it a memorable night. But Ruhi felt completely out of place as she only spoke when spoken to, showing a fake smile to everyone.

Kasim, on the other hand, enjoyed his time with the family. He engaged with Saira, truly showing the families to which they belong. Ruhi occupied herself with Mahirah and Daniyal, staying by their side and avoiding Kasim and Saira.

Ruhi's behavior was noticeable as her usual bubbly charm was gone. After watching Kasim and Saira's interaction, she knew she made the right decision to leave after the engagement. Daniyal and Mahirah saw glimpses of her broken heart, but they kept quiet.

Ruhi truly felt alone, unable to share her pain with anyone.

"Ruhi, is everything okay?" Reshma asked, showing her concern and hugging her.

"Yes. I'm happy that we're all together again." Ruhi said masking her inner turmoil.

"Kasim's not bothering you right? Let's hide behind the bushes and scare him." Daniyal said, laughing, Ruhi smiled a bit, wiping her tears.

The family laughed as they began supper, sharing stories of their childhood, remembering Asma and how happy she would've been. After dinner, Saira went home early, exhausted from the preparations.

Mahirah suddenly felt unwell, and the entire family gathered to attend to her. Kasim and Omar checked her thoroughly, requesting her to retire for the night. Once the situation settled, Ruhi helped clean up, ensuring everything was in place before the night ended.

One by one, the family retired for the night. Ruhi, however, felt restless. So, she walked outside, stepping onto Rehan's lawn, gazing quietly at the moon. She was so lost in thought she didn't notice Kasim approaching. Until it was too late.

The moment her eyes met his, she froze. Kasim's gaze was intense, searching. Ruhi immediately turned away. She decided to leave before he could say anything.

But—

He grabbed her hand, his firm grip holding her wrist as thunder roared in the night sky.

"Let go!" Ruhi's voice was quiet, strained.

"Not until you tell me what's wrong." Kasim's grip tightened slightly.

"Why are you behaving this way?"

"I'm not," Ruhi lied, trying to pull away. "Let go,"

Kasim didn't budge.

"You're being distant," he said, his voice laced with frustration.

"And I need to know why."

Ruhi clenched her jaw.

"Stop worrying about me."

Her voice wavered as she releases herself from his grip.

"It's not your place."

Kasim's brows furrowed.

"What's that supposed to mean?"

"Nothing."

She tried to walk away again—

But once more, Kasim grabbed her, his hands holding her arms tightly as thunder roared and rain began to fall.

Kasim stood his ground, drenched in the rain.

At last, they were facing each other. Kasim is holding her and staring into her eyes. Ruhi was silent, pleading with him to let her go.

"Please—"

"Not until you answer my question."

His dark eyes locked onto hers.

"Tell me *why* you're not happy."

Ruhi turned her face away. She wanted to run, to pretend this conversation wasn't happening.

But Kasim didn't let go.

He pulled her closer holding her, his hands moving slowly from her forearms hold onto her wrist, her palm placed at his chest.

Firm.

Unshaken.

Unrelenting.

"Tell me *why* you're not happy, Ruhi."

Ruhi felt her walls crumbling. Her heart pounded in her chest. Tears welled in her eyes.

And finally—

She broke.

"Because I'm *in* love with you!"

Her voice echoed through the rain. Kasim's expression stilled.

His hands slowly loosened their grip.

He blinked.

Once.

Twice.

"I've been *in* love with you, Kasim."

Ruhi's voice shook, her emotions spilling out like a flood.

"I don't know when it happened or how—but I didn't understand what love was until now.

And now—it's too late."

Kasim suddenly laughed. But there was no joy in it.

Only pain.

"Where was this love seven years ago?"

His voice was calm but sharp as a blade.

"Where was this love when I poured out my heart to you?"

Ruhi flinched as thunder roared.

"You can't keep pulling me toward you when it's convenient

and push me away when it's not."

"I know," she whispered, guilt weighing on her chest.

"I'm sorry."

Kasim let out a slow breath.

Then—

He pulled her close again, his hand on her shoulder gripping her with his every fiber, their faces inches away.

Holding her so tight, she could hear his heartbeat. He stared into her tear-filled eyes, his own stormy with emotion.

THUNDER.

"Why do you love me now?

When I loved you, I just saw you... *all* of you.

I saw your kind heart that you hid from the world.

Let me ask you this, Ruhi, are you *sure* you're in love with me, or do you just *think* you're in love with me?"

DASTAAN -E- ISHQ

THUNDER.

His voice was raw, vulnerable. The unspoken silence filled with the fallen rain as they stared at each other.

"Tell me. *Is it because I'm successful now?*

Or because I'm not *fat* anymore?"

Ruhi's eyes widened in shock.

Kasim's lips curled slightly.

"Am I *finally* good-looking enough for you, is that it?

Now that I have ambition, you want me.

Someone to be your *equal* who looks good by your side,"

His words cut through her like a knife.

"If those are your reasons, then I don't want your love."

THUNDER.

And with that—

He let go.

Ruhi stood there, drenched in the rain, her chest tightening. She had hurt him beyond repair. Her own words from seven years ago came back to haunt her.

Then—

She spoke from her heart.

"I'm *in love* with the man you've *always* been.

The man who puts others before himself.

The man who worked *tirelessly* for his success but never let it *change* him.

The man who remained *loyal*, who always stood by his family. Who applauded my success more than his own.

I'm in love with the same man who loved me years ago."

THUNDER.

She took a shaky breath.

"I was wrong. And I hurt you; I realize that now.

But I need you to know—I've thought of you every single

day for the past seven years."

Her tears mixed with the rain as she finally whispered—

"I love you, Kasim."

Kasim stayed silent.

His hands clenched into fists.

"So, I should break Saira's heart for you?"

THUNDER.

Ruhi's breath hitched.

"Why are you telling me this now?"

Ruhi swallowed.

"I was afraid."

Her voice cracked.

"I thought you'd reject me the way I rejected you."

Kasim laughed again, shaking his head.

DASTAAN -E- ISHQ

"Nothing has changed."

His voice was icy cold.

"Everything *is* about *you. Isn't it?*"

Ruhi froze.

"Did you ever stop to think about how long it took me to get over you?... I loved you with my *whole* heart, Ruhi.

And you broke me!"

THUNDER.

His voice rose slightly, anger flashing in his eyes.

"Today, you've brought *us* back to the same place."

He inhaled sharply.

"I know what it's like to be heartbroken. And I *will* never do that to anyone else.

I'm going to go *through* with the engagement."

THUNDER.

His words echoed in the rain. Ruhi felt his heartbreak in a way she never had before.

She had *lost* him.

Finally—she turned and ran.

Tears streamed down her face as she reached her home, gasping for breath. She stood on her lawn, trembling, soaking in the rain. Her cries howled with the icy wind.

On the other side of the wall stood Kasim on his lawn.

Rain pouring on him.

Crying.

Two people crying in the rain are side by side, separated by a wall.

Two hearts breaking together, their broken hearts masked by the rainfall.

Two souls mourning what they could have been.

***

The day of the engagement had arrived, but Ruhi felt utterly shattered. She never imagined she would confess her love to Kasim, yet it had happened. Her rejection and heartbreak were justified—because she had done the same to Kasim years ago.

Her pain was unbearable, but she knew she had to push through for Saira. Even though she loved Kasim, she would never betray Saira's trust or stand in the way of her happiness. Ruhi had made up her mind. She would leave right after the engagement.

Ruhi stood in the room, packing her suitcases, when Saira entered.

"Where are you going? And why aren't you ready?" Saira asked, frowning.

"There's a fashion show in Dubai. The investors need me there tonight.

I'll leave after the ring ceremony."

Saira sighed but nodded.

"Okay... I'm just glad you'll be here for the ceremony. But

you're still not ready?"

Ruhi forced a small smile and pulled out a random outfit from her suitcase.

"I'll just wear this."

Saira rolled her eyes and walked over to Ruhi's closet.

"No way. I saw this in your closet a few days ago."

She pulled out the lavender and silver outfit Kasim had given her. Ruhi bought the outfit as a trinket of her love.

Ruhi's heart clenched.

"No, I'll wear something else."

"There's nothing else. And this is nice, suits you well...Please, put this on," Saira said with a simile before leaving.

Ruhi stared at the outfit, her hands shaking. This was the last thing Kasim had given her.

Would she ever see him again after today?

Will their friendship survive this test?

Saira, already ready for her engagement, arrives in the room. Ruhi was ready in her lavender silver outfit as she stood helplessly in front of the mirror. Saira insisted on helping her get ready. Ruhi sat her down in front of the vanity mirror, Saira helping her with her makeup and jewelry.

Hours later, the entire family gathered at Kasim's house. Everyone was joyous, excited, celebrating. Ruhi felt like an outsider, truly unhappy, but her smile showed a different story.

Ruhi saw Kasim, happy as ever. She felt the night's events did not affect him but knew she'd be happy for him regardless. Kasim on the other hand avoided her at all costs as Ruhi broke from inside. She kept herself busy with housework, avoiding everyone's eyes.

Mahirah noticed her distress and pulled her aside.

"Did you tell him yet?"

Ruhi swallowed hard.

"There's nothing to tell."

Mahirah shook her head as Daniyal approached the ladies.

Mahirah stood firmly against her, "I can see your pain. You have to speak up before it's too late."

Ruhi forced a fake smile.

"I'm sorry, excuse me."

Her emotions were too much to bear. Daniyal stopped her.

"It's not too late. What are you worried about?

I'll stop this engagement if—"

"No. I can't do this to Kasim and Saira. Please—" Ruhi said, her voice laced with the remanence of her sorrow.

Daniyal and Mahirah understood Ruhi's sacrifice. She loved Kasim enough to let him go, even at the cost of her own happiness.

But did he know?

Had he not noticed the misery she carried?

Their eyes lingered on Kasim as he mingled effortlessly with his guests, seemingly content, unaware—or perhaps unwilling to see—the weight Ruhi bore in silence.

Ruhi noticed Omar and Rehan gathered on the stage. Her eyes followed Kasim as he gently took Saira's hand, helping her up the steps. A sudden wave of heartache surged through her, tightening in her chest, leaving her breathless in silent misery.

As the ring ceremony was about to begin, Ruhi walked around, trying to clear her mind hoping no one would notice her leaving as Reshma approached her.

"Ruhi, you have to take the rings on the stage."

Ruhi nodded, masking her tears with a smile. She picked up the tray with the rings. A single tear fell onto the tray. She quickly wiped it away and took a deep breath. Her heart was pounding painfully in her chest.

She walked without confidence as a flashback of Kasim flooded her mind. Her tears fell on the tray. But she knew his happiness was with Saira now, and she *had* to accept it.

As she walked to the stage, she heard Rehan say—

"Oh, look, Ruhi brought the rings," Rehan said as Omar, Reshma, and Kiran approached the stage.

Ruhi's heartache was visible on her face but was disregarded by her family.

"Go ahead, put the ring on her finger! What's the hold-up?"

Ruhi felt her heart shatter all over again. She couldn't take it. She turned to leave.

Suddenly—

A hand grabbed hers.

Ruhi froze.

For a moment, she thought it was a dream. She felt paralyzed, unable to turn around.

But then—she did.

And she saw Kasim.

Holding her hand.

The room erupted into cheers. Taking the ring out of the box.

Ruhi's eyes widened in shock. Kasim pulled her close gently.

"You think I'll let you go again?"

He slides the engagement ring on her finger. Saira smiled with relief.

"Thank God... For a minute there, I was worried I had to go through this engagement."

Ruhi's breath hitched.

"Did you really think I would go get engaged to Saira?

When I love you and only you." Kasim asked, his voice soft, full of emotion.

Ruhi was speechless. Tears fell freely from her eyes.

"Why?" she whispered.

Kasim smiled softly, wiping a tear from her cheek.

"Because I wanted you to see the *real* me.

Not my success, my looks, or my career.

Only me.

I have always admired your courage more than your ambition.

I always knew *you* were the only one for me.

I knew you were lost, just like I was. And you found me; you made me whole again.

I knew you loved me, but you would never let go of your guilt of what happened seven years ago.

So, I had to do this. To make *you* realize your own feelings.

Otherwise, you would've ran."

Ruhi turned to Saira, tears still falling. Saira smiled warmly.

"I've always known you two were meant for each other. I would *never* do anything to hurt you.

I had no intention of marrying Kasim.

Believe me.

It's true, over the years, we became good friends, but that's all it is.

Yes, we talked every day, and he only asked about *you*.

He gave me tips on how to handle you, how to talk to you."

Kasim chuckled softly.

Ruhi's heart swelled.

"You're a good friend, Saira. Only a real friend would do this for me... I'm truly sorry; I never meant to hurt you in any of this," Kasim said sincerely.

Saira laughed.

"I wanted to do this for both of you. Besides, I would have been hurt if I didn't know the truth.

Plus—anything for my best friends."

Ruhi hugged Saira tightly, crying.

"Thank you."

Rehan and Omar stepped forward.

"I know we played our part in this. For that, I am sorry. I knew how you felt the day you came back from the orphanage.

I was happy our dream finally came true.

We wanted you to be part of our family; you're our first and only choice," Rehan admitted.

"But… we were afraid that history would repeat itself. We didn't want to force anything on you kids." Rehan continued.

Omar nodded. "We wanted to make sure you were ready for this decision, that you both made together. We were willing to wait however long we needed to."

Daniyal stood proudly with his brother.

"Ruhi, life doesn't give people second chances easily. In the last seven years, you both lost parts of yourself that only the two of you could find."

"We just wanted to bring you two together; we didn't mean to hurt you in the process," said Mahirah.

Reshma wiped her tears. "I'm glad my son chose you, Ruhi.

I've known you belong with Kasim since you both were five years old.

I wanted this to be *your* choice not ours."

Kiran interjected. "From the moment you both woke up, you wanted to be in each other's company. And we knew one day you'd create a family together."

Omar smiled at Kasim.

"I always saw potential in you, even when you didn't see it yourself. I know you're the only man that'll balance my daughter out.

But I wanted to be sure.

That's why I asked you to care for her after her injury. Hoping you'll reunite us.

And you proved *me* right."

Omar gently takes Kasim's engagement ring out of the box and hands it to Ruhi. He gave his blessing as he kissed her forehead.

Kasim leaned in close to Ruhi, whispering:

"You'll never know how much I truly love you."

Ruhi smiled through her tears.

"I have an idea...And you'll never know how incomplete I am without you."

With trembling hands, she placed the ring on his finger.

The guests erupted into applause. Right then, Daniyal, Mahirah, Kiran, and Reshma asked a Kazi attending the engagement to perform the Nikka a marriage ceremony. Omar and Rehan agree without hesitation.

At last, Kasim and Ruhi were one.

Their love—eternal and unwavering—was built on understanding, respect, communication, and loyalty. Through every challenge, they had learned one simple truth:

When it's true love, everything falls into place at the right time. They knew this.

And that's where their story truly began.

You'll know it in your soul when its

real....

DASTAAN -E- ISHQ

ABOUT THE AUTHOR

I, Aarhaan S. Bhatti, am a passionate storyteller whose imagination knows no bounds. With a love for crafting tales that transport readers to other realms, I weave together adventure, romance, human emotion, mystery, and wonder elements. Inspired by a lifelong fascination with books and literature. I enjoy creating rich, immersive worlds filled with vibrant characters and compelling narratives. When not lost in imagination, I can often explore nature or be lost in a good book, seeking inspiration for the next adventure to share with readers.

DASTAAN -E- ISHQ

DASTAAN -E- ISHQ

DASTAAN -E- ISHQ

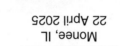

8e68c2213-1eef-4b54-9716-29bcc7d21b24R01